"We need to... this weekend."

"But I—I've only just started working here," Amber began incredulously.

"This is not an ideal situation, I grant you, but it will help me clarify a certain issue." He bent and picked up a piece of paper from the floor and held it out to her. "Do you always work in such a mess?"

"What issue?" Amber avoided the last, far-too-awkward question.

"The issue of whether you are competent enough to be my personal assistant."

"But you'll be throwing me in at the deep end!" Amber protested. "That's not...fair!"

"Fair?" For once Michael Hamilton looked genuinely perplexed. "What's 'fair' got to do with anything? This is business." He began strolling toward his office door. "How's your doggy paddle, Miss King? Sink or swim. I wonder which it will be?"

Laura Martin lives in a small Gloucestershire village, in England, with her husband, two young children and a lively sheepdog! Laura has a great love of interior design and, together with her husband, has recently completed the renovation of their Victorian cottage. Her hobbies include gardening, the theater, music and reading, and she finds great pleasure and inspiration from walking daily in the beautiful countryside around her home.

Falling for the Boss
Laura Martin

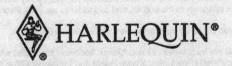

TORONTO • NEW YORK • LONDON
AMSTERDAM • PARIS • SYDNEY • HAMBURG
STOCKHOLM • ATHENS • TOKYO • MILAN • MADRID
PRAGUE • WARSAW • BUDAPEST • AUCKLAND

ISBN 0-373-17436-5

FALLING FOR THE BOSS

First North American Publication 1999.

Copyright © 1997 by Laura Martin.

This edition published by arrangement with Harlequin Books S.A.

® and TM are trademarks of the publisher. Trademarks indicated with ® are registered in the United States Patent and Trademark Office, the Canadian Trade Marks Office and in other countries.

Look us up on-line at: http://www.romance.net

Printed in U.S.A.

CHAPTER ONE

'AMBER, are you crazy? Michael Hamilton is no fool; in fact he's a wolf in wolf's clothing with a mind like a steel trap! He'll see through you in less than no time!'

'No, he won't!' Amber smiled reassuringly at her stepsister, who was lounging miserably on her double bed, clutching a very soggy handkerchief. 'I'm not walking into this with my eyes closed. I've done my groundwork.' She held the smart navy suit against her slim body and eyed herself critically in the full-length mirror. 'What do you think? It's not exactly me, is it?'

'Far too smart,' Beatrice replied morosely. 'And it looks expensive. Where did you get it?' she added suspiciously.

'Borrowed!' Amber announced with satisfaction. 'Remember Carol, who left university after half a term and went on to run her own advertising agency? She's got a wardrobe that's practically the size of this room. Rows and rows of executive-style suits in all colours—'

'You didn't!'

'I did. Why not?' Slender shoulders were lifted in a casual shrug. 'She didn't mind at all. In fact she was rather taken with the whole idea. Carol always was a bit of a tearaway.' Amber scooped up her wild coppery tresses. 'Hair up, do you think? It looks more sophisticated, I suppose...'

She spun around when her sister made no reply and released a small sigh. 'Oh, do stop looking so disapproving, Bea!' she added swiftly. 'Carol didn't mind a bit when I asked to borrow some of her clothes. What's wrong in turning to a friend when you need some help?' Striking golden

5

eyes, the colour of her name, rested on her stepsister's blotchy face and Amber silently cursed Michael Hamilton for the hundredth time. 'You turned to me, didn't you?'

Beatrice sighed. 'I phoned you for a bit of support. I never expected you to get so worked up and go to these lengths!' She bit down worriedly on her bottom lip. 'Michael Hamilton is a powerful man—a ruthless one too. I don't want you to get into trouble because of…of my problems. Don't you think this plan of yours is just going to make matters a whole lot worse?'

'How can they be worse?' Amber asked bluntly, looking deep into the red-rimmed eyes. She brushed a tendril of hair back from her sister's face. She did love her so. Beatrice was such a sweet-natured girl.

Amber could still remember that moment when they had been anxiously introduced to one another. Such opposites, but they had liked each other from the first moment, loved each other soon after that. It had been good to have someone to share things with, for Amber to know that after so much grief her mother was happy again. And Beatrice's father was a good man—not as wonderful as her own dear father, but kind and humorous and understanding, especially about Amber's determination to continue using her own name, even after her mother's marriage.

Which was just as well, Amber thought now with relief, for this evil employer of Beatrice's might become just a trifle suspicious if she went for an interview sharing the same surname as her stepsister.

'Oh, Bea, stop looking so worried, will you? Michael Hamilton has treated you dreadfully and you know it!' she continued forcefully. 'I've never seen you so upset. You're not prepared to do anything about that lecherous swine, but I can…or at least I can try!' Amber swallowed as a flash of anger ran through her body again. 'He can't be allowed to get away with it, Bea; treating people as if they're little more than possessions to dispose of at will! It's not right. There are laws against sexual harassment!'

'He didn't exactly harass me—' Beatrice began.

'He propositioned you, though, didn't he? And you told me he made life pretty difficult for you when you refused his advances. He must have, or else why would you have resigned so suddenly?'

Amber rose from the floor, missing her sister's worried frown. 'Carol gave me a fabulous reference too; did I tell you? Lots of talk about integrity and reliability. I almost began believing I really had worked for her! Thank goodness I struggled all the way through that typing and shorthand course, and my French isn't bad either. It looks like both things are going to come in useful, doesn't it?'

'Only if you get the job,' Bea replied. 'And, to be honest, Amber, I just can't see you managing it. I know you fancy yourself as a good amateur actress, but being a PA to someone like Michael Hamilton, even if it is only a temporary post, isn't going to be easy!' Beatrice lifted her hands in a gesture of helplessness. 'You won't have a clue where to start. And…and what about your friend Carol? Won't she get into the most awful trouble? A phoney reference has to be classed as fraud or…or *something*!'

Amber pursed her lips resolutely. The consequences, should she be found out, were not something she proposed to dwell on. Be positive. That had always been her motto and it had stood her in good stead up to now. She released a small sigh. Just as well too. The last few months had been a bit of a disaster; she had scraped through university with a reasonable degree and had hoped to find a post teaching, but so far every job she'd gone for had fallen through. It was enough to make the strongest character crumble.

'Don't worry; I can pick it up as I go along,' she declared confidently, slipping the navy tailored jacket off its hanger and thrusting her arms into the sleeves. 'I always was a fast learner.'

'Be warned! Michael is a stickler for efficiency,' Beatrice murmured. 'He's as hard as nails. Anyone who doesn't make the grade is in for a tough time.'

'Really?' Amber kept her gaze fixed on the mirror. 'What sort of "tough" are we talking here?'

'Grade A tough! A complete dressing down and then out on your ear without a second chance. He knows how to humiliate.' Beatrice sniffed morosely. 'Believe me, Michael Hamilton can annihilate a person's self-esteem with just a few carefully chosen words.'

'Oh, Bea! Don't let what happened with the swine upset you any more, he's just not worth it.'

'But—'

'And you don't have to worry about me!' Amber forced herself to sound more confident than she felt. 'I can take care of myself. I know you think this is a crazy idea, but it's got to be better than sitting around doing nothing, hasn't it?'

Anything had to be better than that.

'You can do this! You are an able, amateur actress. The drama society at university practically cried when you graduated. This is just another role. Think efficient. Think mature and sophisticated.'

Amber tipped her head back and looked up at the tall glass building which shimmered in the heat of a particularly warm late spring day. It certainly emphasised the wealth of the Hamilton Corporation construction empire, she thought, desperately trying to ignore the churning mass of nerves in her stomach. It was as swish as any in the heart of the city. An edifice that oozed power and success.

She took a steadying breath and walked towards the glittering building, glancing nervously at her watch. Five minutes before her interview. Did she look all right? She had spent ages on her appearance, making sure every detail was just right, but putting on this suit and crisp white shirt, slipping her feet into the smart shoes with their small block heels, had felt totally alien. Her hair felt wrong too; taming the unruly strands into such a tidy coil at the nape of her neck had been an absolute nightmare.

Amber hesitated at the swing-doors, pausing to glance at her reflection in the mirrored glass which covered the whole of the building. Drat! Her hair was escaping already.

She placed her large, briefcase-style bag onto the tiled floor of the outer entrance and hastily began smoothing and cajoling the fiery strands back into place. If she didn't do something about it straight away, she knew she would look like the wild woman from the west by the time of her interview.

Amber stepped back to get a better view in the reflective tinted glass and in the next moment she was suffering the indignity of lying flat on her back, with her skirt halfway up her thighs and a good deal of smooth, stockinged flesh on display.

'For goodness' sake!'

Stunned by the unexpected collision, Amber looked up in dazed stupefaction. She saw a dark suit, the flash of a patterned silk tie, and then a large hand was reaching down and in a second she was being yanked unceremoniously to her feet.

'What a stupid place to stand!'

She didn't like the voice; it might have been deep and resonant, with an attractive husky edge, but the tone, the *way* she was being spoken to, was totally infuriating.

Amber tilted her chin automatically and glared. 'You should have looked where you were going!'

Ice-blue eyes penetrated her face. The firm, well-shaped

mouth hardened into an even firmer line. 'Should I, indeed?'

She gulped hard, then met the challenge in his gaze. He was tall, dark and quite heart-stoppingly handsome, but she wasn't going to let that make a scrap of difference. 'Yes!' she snapped, smoothing her skirt down hastily over her slim hips. 'You should! I could have been knocked out cold.'

Sharp, intelligent eyes raked her figure in a swift, all-seeing appraisal and then came to rest with cool precision on her face. 'But you weren't, were you?' The attractive mouth fashioned itself into a smile. 'How fortunate.'

Did he care? Amber drew in a deep breath and decided that he didn't. Not a jot. The only emotions discernible in his face were cool irritation and impatience, coupled with the faintest impression of amusement.

'You could at least apologise.' Amber pursed her lips defiantly and did her best to ignore the embarrassment of the situation. Several passers-by had seen her undignified fall and a couple were, she noticed, watching the subsequent conversation with interest. 'I banged my elbow hard and it hurts...a *lot*!' she added crossly.

'I apologise.' The watchful blue eyes were special. When used in conjunction with the smooth, deep voice, they were positively lethal. The man took a pace towards her, his gaze intent on the sleeve of Amber's jacket. 'Let me take a look at the damage.'

'No!' She hurriedly manoeuvred and sidestepped out of his way. 'It's fine!'

'A moment ago you said it was hurting a great deal. Now that's what I call a swift recovery.'

The sarcasm in his voice made her blood boil. She decided on the honest, uncaring approach. 'OK, so I lied!'

'Did you, indeed?'

'Yes.' Amber lifted her chin defiantly. 'I did. Look,' she added airily, 'I can't stand chatting here all day. I've got things to do.' She made as if to go round him, but his broad frame blocked her path.

'People to see?'

He was mocking her. Deep down she decided reluctantly that she couldn't blame him. Usually, when anyone bumped into her, she was the first to apologise. What was she being so...so disagreeable for now? 'That's right,' she replied crisply. 'And I'm going to be late.'

'You'll need this.' He bent down and picked up Amber's bag, which was lying sprawled at his feet, and held it out in front of her with hands that were large and tanned and somehow incredibly sexy. 'Yours, presumably.'

'Thank you!' She reached out to remove the bag from his grasp, but just as she thought she had sole possession of it she felt the straps being jerked away from her and in the next moment she was being tugged against an extremely solid chest.

She gasped, then looked up. He was tall—taller than she had at first imagined—and more powerful too; up close her small frame seemed to be enveloped by the width of his chest. Heat rushed through Amber's body as a large hand was raised to her face. She could smell the discreet scent of his cologne, could see the fine lines around his eyes, the fringe of thick dark lashes. She told herself she should move; she *wanted* to move, but somehow her brain's ability to order her limbs into motion had become diminished by this sudden outrageous occurrence.

Get a grip! Amber scolded herself. She gulped a swift breath, remembering somewhat belatedly that she had a voice and was capable of speech. She glanced up in angry astonishment. 'What do you think you're doing?'

'Our collision has messed up your hair. It needs putting right.' Strong fingers brushed an errant strand from her face and tucked it behind her ear. 'After all, you look as if you're dressed for something important; it would be a shame to ruin the effect.'

The tone was different now—smooth and seductive and extremely dangerous. Amber gulped in shock as the mouth curved expressively and came just a fraction closer.

Did this man possess some sort of hypnotic skill? she wondered dazedly. One per cent of her mind was screaming, *Interview! Interview!*, whilst the other ninety-nine per cent was only concerned with what was going to happen next... How daring he would be. How daring she *wanted* him to be.

He was playing with her. She knew it, but somehow it didn't seem to make any difference. Her body burned with a confused jumble of emotions: dislike and attraction, irritation and reluctant admiration.

'I can do it!' She finally remembered that she was capable of movement too, and drew back, anxious fingers moving erratically to smooth her hair away from her face. She glanced at her watch in a typically nervous gesture and cursed softly beneath her breath.

'You're late?'

She glanced up and saw the dark brows raised in mild, amused query.

'Yes,' Amber replied stiffly, working hard to assume a more assured tone. She glanced around absent-mindedly for her bag and realised that the stranger opposite was still holding it. 'If you wouldn't mind?' She held out her hand in a no-nonsense gesture and waited with cold impatience until her bag was returned to her.

'Do you work here?'

She followed his gaze, was aware of smart, impeccably dressed men and women passing by them to enter or leave the building. 'I...I have business here,' Amber replied evasively. She flashed the tanned, handsome face a pointed look. 'Do you?'

'Work here?' There was a slight pause; the attractive, dangerous mouth firmed slightly. 'It has been known.' His dark voice was suddenly icy and impersonal. Competent fingers flicked back the cuff of his shirt and glanced at a gleaming Rolex watch. 'And, as it happens, I too am behind schedule, and all because you decided you just *had* to attend to your hair!'

Her mouth dropped open as the casual male arrogance resurfaced once again. 'But that wasn't my fault—!' she began, determined not to let him get away with such a blatantly unfair remark.

He cut through her remonstrations crisply. 'I'm afraid that, much as I am enjoying this riveting conversation, I cannot stop to chat any longer. Mundane but vital business awaits.' The attractive mouth curved mockingly. 'Maybe we'll bump into each other again—figuratively speaking, of course.'

And with that he was gone, striding confidently through the swing-doors of the building without a backward glance, leaving Amber alone on the pavement, feeling cross and cheated and quite curiously empty.

'Miss King?' A sour, middle-aged woman eyed Amber suspiciously as she hurriedly approached the clinically austere waiting area, which didn't have another human soul in it. 'You're late. Mr Hamilton does not like to be kept waiting.'

'Yes...I'm dreadfully sorry,' Amber puffed. As usual she had declined the speed of the lift for the less claustrophobic qualities of the stairs and was still out of breath. 'I had a bit of trouble—'

The woman wasn't interested. Thin lips pursed disapprovingly, and a brittle, efficient voice cut through Amber's hasty explanation. 'Please take a seat. I'll find out if Mr Hamilton can still see you. He left his office a moment ago to visit another part of the building.'

Amber sat on a black leather sofa and stared at the vast sea of pale grey carpet which seemed to occupy every inch of highly valued floor space. I've blown it, she thought despondently, even before I set foot in the interview. Good going, girl! You really know how to give yourself a fighting chance.

Now what would she tell Bea? Despite all her sister's protestations Amber felt sure she would want her to succeed. At least the despairing look had disappeared, even if it had only been replaced by nervous anxiety and anticipation.

Damn Michael Hamilton! If he refused to see her now, just because she was a few minutes late... Amber glanced at her wrist-watch. Well, more than just a few minutes, more like a quarter of an hour. But even so—

'Miss King!' Sourpuss was back and her expression wasn't any more welcoming. Amber looked across at the desk and stood up without a great deal of hope. 'Would you come this way, please?'

Was she going to get her chance after all? Amber didn't know whether to feel relieved or not as she followed a few paces behind the formidable-looking woman. They traversed a wide, plushly carpeted corridor and arrived at some heavy double doors.

'Mr Hamilton will be with you shortly.' The doors were opened ceremoniously by the elderly woman and Amber was gestured across the threshold. 'Please take a seat.'

There was a hushed, almost reverential silence. The strong sun and sticky heat of the outside world, the bustle of people toing and froing in the main concourse seemed a world away from this inner sanctum on the top floor.

This was power and wealth, Amber mused as the doors were pulled closed behind her. This quiet, discreetly furnished office with its tasteful pieces of art and heavy, glossy wood bore the unmistakable signs of someone who was a complete and utter success. It was the place from where an autocratic, self-important, arrogant man by the name of Michael Hamilton ruled his empire…

A thought speared her mind. A thought so incredibly outrageous that it was too awful to contemplate. Amber shook her head. No, no, it couldn't be. She was allowing her imagination to run away with her. She swallowed and found her mouth as dry as a desert. Calm down, she told herself. It wouldn't be him. Fate or coincidence or whatever it was that governed the way things worked out couldn't be that cruel.

She released a steadying breath and tried to get her thoughts into some kind of order. But now that the possibility had entered her head she didn't seem to be able to think straight. Her twisted mind kept whispering awful possibilities—what ifs that were too ridiculous to believe.

Michael Hamilton was an old man, or older at least. Amber had built up a picture in her mind. Sleek and repugnantly oily. A craggy, unforgiving face with a hooked nose.

It was pure imagination, of course; Bea had told her little about his physical appearance. In truth, she had never been one to talk much about her work. And then, after she had handed in her resignation, she had been too upset to offer much in the way of details.

Amber's mouth firmed into a determined line. Damn swine! Trying to seduce her sister! Forcing his oily attentions on Bea, who was far too naïve for her own good. Well, she'd show him! She'd teach him a lesson he'd never forget! Just let him try the same sort of treatment on her!

Her heart was thundering like a steam train. If Michael Hamilton dared to walk in now, she didn't think she'd be able to restrain herself.

But he didn't. Time ticked by. Amber worked hard at calming her over-zealous temper. She focused golden eyes on the desk ahead of her. Papers were arranged neatly on the blotter. There was an organiser laid open with sharp black writing marking the lined pages. A Chinese vase had a neat selection of pens and pencils jammed into it. She rose from her seat and was just about to pick the porcelain up, to see if it really was as expensive as it looked, when she heard the door being opened behind her.

She spun around sharply, knocking the object with her elbow as she turned, and listened with a sinking heart as the vase bounced on the plush carpet, and the pens and pencils scattered messily at her feet.

But she didn't bend to pick them up. She didn't move. She stood transfixed, staring dumbly across the vast expanse of office space, all thoughts of the vase forgotten, all thoughts of *anything* forgotten, staring with eyes as round as saucers and a heart that thundered fit to burst.

'Is it broken?'

So fate had decided to be cruel. To test her—*really* test her.

Crisp, dark suit, patterned silk tie...

Michael Hamilton stood in the doorway, watching her.

His voice held no hint of surprise; it was deep and inflexible and precise, matching the sharp, dark suited image. 'Well? You really are rather accident-prone, aren't you, Miss King?' He walked towards her, with slow, measured steps that brought him within touching distance. 'Didn't you hear what I said? Is it broken?'

Amber gulped a breath. Slowly her senses were beginning to return. She glanced down at the vase on the floor, as if seeing it for the first time, and hastily bent to retrieve it, placing it back onto the polished desk with fingers that shook visibly. 'No...no.' She bent again and with trembling fingers gathered the pens and pencils from around her feet. 'No...no, it's not.'

'Just as well. Your chances of getting this post would be severely reduced if you had broken a three-thousand-pound antique. Leave them!' He placed a large, restraining hand over Amber's fingers as she clumsily tried to return the writing implements to their home. 'I don't want it hitting the floor a second time—you might not be so lucky then.'

He wasn't amused. That fact, along with the scorch of his touch, registered as Michael Hamilton rounded his desk. Hell! He looked intimidating. Outside had been nothing; he had been positively playful compared with the way he was now. A narrowing of the eyes, a slight firming of the well-shaped mouth—that was all it took.

Amber gulped in a lungful of air and wondered whether there was any point staying in the room. It seemed unlikely. Here she was, applying for a highly responsible post, a position that demanded efficiency and tact and intelligence...

She grimaced and then looked up. Sharp blue eyes were surveying her face. Michael Hamilton was reading her mind. 'Not exactly the best of starts, is it, Miss King?' he announced crisply. 'I should imagine you're wishing you could turn the clock back and begin again.'

'It would make things a lot easier,' Amber agreed stiffly. 'You don't seem particularly surprised to see me in your office,' she added, determined not to be totally undermined by this dominating individual. 'Were you aware that I was an applicant for the post of personal assistant when we... er...met outside?'

'It crossed my mind.'

'Before or after you collided with me?' she asked pertly, annoyed by his casual reply.

'There was a lot of traffic outside the office this lunch-time,' he drawled with lazy assurance. 'I had my chauffeur drop me further along the street. I watched you cross the road. I noticed the way you held yourself, the way you looked up at the building.' His attractive mouth curved slightly. 'Body language is a useful thing. It can reveal a great deal about a person.' He paused momentarily. 'It tells me now that you're not used to dressing so smartly. I suggest you leave your suit alone, Miss King. You look fine.'

Amber balled her hands into fists at her sides. 'I...I'm a little nervous, that's all,' she answered swiftly. 'I...I didn't expect things to turn out so...so awkwardly.'

'Turn out?' The mouth was curved, mocking her again. 'But we haven't even started, Miss King. There's a long way to go yet, I do assure you.' He gestured negligently with his hand. 'Sit down.'

She sat. She should have told Michael Hamilton what to do with his job and walked straight out of his office, but she didn't.

Amber smoothed her skirt with trembling fingers, noticed his penetrating gaze, checked herself and laid her hands demurely in her lap.

It was probably pointless now, but all that preparation... She couldn't give in without some sort of effort. Think of Bea, she told herself. Think of Bea, who was forced to resign after years of hard work because she couldn't bear to work with this dominating individual a moment longer.

Get this job, Amber King, and then you'll be able to work on a plan to exact revenge.

CHAPTER TWO

AMBER steeled herself and then, with a determined expression fixed on her face, stood up, approached the desk and held out her hand, concentrating like fury on playing her part.

Go on! Disarm him! Charm him! She flashed a smile—her best feature. Underused so far but capable—or so she had been told—of ensnaring men at thirty paces. 'Look, I'm sorry for the unfortunate start, Mr Hamilton,' she murmured smoothly. 'Could we begin again, do you think? I had no idea who you were outside, and—'

'If you had, you would have behaved differently?'

Amber thought about it. Her chin lifted a few degrees higher. Sorry, Bea, she thought, I'm about to let you down.

'No,' she replied crisply, 'I don't think I would.'

'I see.'

Did he? She hoped not. Infiltrating Michael Hamilton's empire was probably a stupid idea anyway. What had she possibly thought she'd achieve?

He glanced up, an amused smile flickering at the corners of his mouth. 'I accept your apology, Miss King. I'm not the sort of man who holds a grudge. You can consider the slate as being wiped clean.'

Then a large, tanned hand was extended across the desk, and for the third time physical contact was made. He had that kind of aura—you counted the touches.

Maybe just in case they never happened again...

It was a firm, no-nonsense grip. There was no hint in the contact he offered this time of anything other than a cool professionalism, but unfortunately that didn't seem to make any difference…

Drat! Amber thought crossly. Michael Hamilton was having a quite peculiar effect on her. Who was she kidding? she added silently as she retook her seat. Ever since she had set eyes on him, it had been as if a bomb had exploded and she was suffering from shell-shock.

'Your application form is impressive. On paper you have all the things I am looking for in a personal assistant. On paper…' The repetition signified a thousand and one misgivings. She was surveyed once again with cool azure eyes. 'Of course, academic qualifications are meaningless without the right sort of personal qualities.'

He paused, his gaze returning momentarily to the carefully crafted and totally fictional application form that Amber had spent so much time on. 'Why do you want to work for me, Miss King?'

The directness of his question, plus the underlying fear she had of being found out, plus the fact that Michael Hamilton had to be the most handsome, most disturbing man she had ever set eyes on caused Amber's thought processes to shut down. Her mind reeled as all of her rehearsed replies flew straight out of the window.

She stared ahead, mesmerised by the stunning eyes, dumbstruck for several long seconds, knowing she had gone over and over the answer to this question a hundred times before in the privacy of her flat, but finding herself unable to form a single syllable now that she was here, in his office, where it mattered.

I didn't prepare well enough, she thought dazedly.

'Miss King?' There was a narrowing of the eyes, a thread of impatience in the cool, dark voice. 'Are you capable of answering the question?'

She felt like throttling him. She watched, fuming inwardly as he leant back in his black leather chair and rested his elbows nonchalantly on the arms. Such arrogance! Totally inbuilt too. That look, the smooth, unhurried movements were as natural to Michael Hamilton as walking or talking…or making love…

Damn! What had she thought of that for? Michael Hamilton as a lover—where had that thought come from? Not *her* lover, of course—never that! Just let him lay so much as one finger on her and he'd regret it soon enough…

You're losing it! a small voice warned inside her head. Do you want this job or not? Don't think, you fool! Just *act*! Curse her vivid imagination! It would be the finish of her. Michael Hamilton as a lover was an image that was hard to dispel now that it was in her mind.

She did her best. Amber forced a vision of Bea, crying and distraught, into her mind and managed somehow to talk warmly and sincerely about broadening horizons and extending potential and using all of her abilities to their fullest extent.

A dark brow was raised quizzically. She thought she had sounded rather good. Surely Michael Hamilton wasn't still laughing at her behind that enigmatic gaze, was he?

'And those abilities are…?'

She matched his studied observation with a serious look of her own. 'Apart from my academic qualifications,' she replied, getting into her stride now, 'I possess good organisational skills. I've got a healthy measure of common sense and I can assess and deal with any given situation at a moment's notice.'

His mouth curved slightly and her irritation rose. He *was* laughing at her!

'Similar to the way you dealt with our collision earlier, do you mean?'

Amber's lips firmed. 'I don't think you're being entirely fair, Mr Hamilton,' she murmured.

'No?'

'If I were your personal assistant my behaviour would be totally professional,' she added coolly.

'So you're telling me that your display of bad temper was a one-off?'

There was a slight pause whilst Amber struggled quietly with her rage. 'Absolutely. I have a very placid nature,' she lied. 'Many people comment on it.'

'Sounds too good to be true.'

Her heart jolted at his words. 'Not at all.' She parted her carefully painted lips in a sweet smile. 'I have my faults, just like everyone else.'

'And they are…?' The question was casual enough, but she could sense the interest in the deep voice. He twisted the plush swivel chair towards the window a little and then glanced back to survey her with open consideration. 'Care to tell me?'

A flush stained her cheeks as Bea's dire warnings about fraud filled her mind. She inhaled a steadying breath and thrust them determinedly away. 'I have a tendency to be bossy.'

There was a pause. It lengthened. Amber kept her gaze straight ahead, working hard at keeping her composure. Finally, when the silence had grown to almost embarrassing proportions, a dark brow was raised expressively.

'That's it?'

She lifted her shoulders in a slight shrug. There were any number of faults she could tell him about, but admitting that she had a crazy sense of humour or that she shrieked and threw inanimate objects when tiredness and temper got the better of her was, she knew, not going to get her the job. 'No.' Her mouth slanted provocatively. 'But that's all I'm prepared to admit to!'

Was the old Amber charm working? Hell! It was difficult to tell with this man. She had absolutely no idea what he was thinking.

'And vices? What about those?'

'No...I...er...' Her voice trailed to a halt. *Vices?* He was talking to her about vices? She glared at him.

'Presumably you do have some?' Michael Hamilton asked smoothly. 'Most people do.' The attractive mouth widened into a heart-stopping smile. 'Even me.'

Oh, I bet you do! she thought swiftly. I *bet* you do!

'Perhaps you'd tell me if any of them are likely to interfere with your work?' he continued. 'Just for the record.'

Gorging on cream cakes whenever she felt fed up? Refusing to wash up for days on end, so that the sink overflowed and there weren't any plates left in the cupboards? Eating ice cream straight from the carton? Hardly the sort of bad habits that would infringe on the work of a PA. Nothing serious. Nothing that would register on *his* scale.

'I don't smoke, Mr Hamilton, and I drink alcohol in absolute moderation,' Amber responded neutrally. 'I'm not a kleptomaniac or a...a habitual liar.' She felt the flush of guilt warm her cheeks as the last few words fell out of her mouth before they could be retrieved, and wondered if she looked as uneasy as she felt.

'I'm relieved to hear it.' Cool blue eyes raked her face impassively.

Any minute, Amber thought weakly, and he's going to stand up, accuse me of gross fraud and throw me out of his office. She twisted her fingers together in her lap and then released them suddenly as the pain of her nails digging into her flesh registered. 'And boyfriends?'

She gulped a breath. 'I don't believe in allowing my personal life to affect my professional career if that's what you mean, Mr Hamilton!' Her reply came out sounding suitably crisp. She almost added that her personal life was none of his business anyway, but decided that that would be going a little too far.

'What sort of relationship do you consider there should

be between a personal assistant and the head of a large company?'

The answer flew into her head without the slightest effort. Maybe she hadn't lost it completely after all. 'An open, interactive one with each side showing the other mutual respect,' she replied firmly.

The stunning features remained impassive, but she sensed somehow that he approved of her answer. 'Do you have any kind of domestic ties, Miss King? An aged parent? A live-in lover?'

Her head jerked up slightly. 'Pardon? I don't see—'

'This post involves a certain level of commitment, Miss King. I'm sure you are aware of that.'

'Of course.'

'I need a PA who does not have domestic ties which may interfere with her duties.' There was a slight pause and the dark brows drew together in a frown. 'I've never seen such a turnaround in such a short space of time.'

Amber frowned. 'I beg your pardon?'

He looked across at her and the furrow in his brow increased. 'My former personal assistant, who was, up until a few weeks ago, totally committed, left at extremely short notice.'

'Oh…' Amber hesitated, and then added with deliberate casualness, 'What happened?'

'I have no idea. She just walked into my office one day and told me she was leaving. No explanations, no warning, nothing.' He imparted the information with something approaching bemused disbelief.

'Are you sure?'

Sharp eyes focused on her face. 'Of course I'm sure.'

'I mean about why she left,' Amber replied swiftly. She knew she was treading on dangerous ground, but she persisted in spite of, or rather because of, the man opposite. 'There must have been a reason. A problem.' The edge of dislike was difficult to wipe from her voice. 'Maybe something serious…?'

He didn't show his anger, but she guessed it was there, lurking beneath the surface, waiting to bite. After all, she had virtually accused him of failing in his duty as an employer. She longed to say more, *much* more—the words 'arrogant' and 'swine' kept hovering at the forefront of her mind—but Amber summoned the will-power from somewhere and remained silent.

'Miss Davies had ample opportunity to tell me of anything that may have been troubling her,' he replied curtly. 'We'd worked together for long enough for her to have realised that she could come to me with any problem she may have had.'

Liar! Amber thought. How could he sit there and say those things and look as if he meant every word? How easy it was for him! Practice, she supposed. Masses and masses of practice. After all, he surely hadn't got to the position he was in now by being nice or playing by the rules? That would be too much to believe.

'Maybe this will illustrate the necessity of my making enquiries into your social life now,' he continued crisply. 'I require a personal assistant who is level-headed, reliable, efficient, willing to make sacrifices, committed. Someone who can travel or work unsociable hours at a moment's notice—'

'An absolute paragon, by the sounds of it,' Amber replied drily. 'Look, I'll work hard,' she continued quickly. 'Very hard. But if you're looking for a doormat, someone who'll say, Yes, sir, no, sir, three bags full, sir, then I'm afraid we may as well end this interview right here!' She stood up. It was over. She couldn't take this sort of tension any more. It had been a stupid idea anyway… 'I have a life, Mr Hamilton,' she continued. 'One that I quite enjoy

living. I don't intend for it to be completely annihilated just
because—'

'Sit down!'

His voice was firm and cool, cutting effectively through
her heated words. Amber stared at the enigmatic face for a
long moment and then, without dwelling on the significance
of her action, retook her seat.

Michael Hamilton considered her silently for a moment.
A long, searching look that was unnerving, to say the least.
Amber forced herself to meet his gaze. Did she detect intrigue, interest, maybe just a little amusement lurking in the
handsome features?

'I can accept what you've just said, Miss King,' he continued. 'You are a young, attractive woman and I'm not
about to tell you that you cannot have a private life—that
would be totally unrealistic. But you must also see that it
would be preferable if personal relationships—romantic or
otherwise—didn't dominate. You must realise that this is a
responsible position. I rely, heavily at times, on the efficiency and commitment of my personal assistant.' Amber
wished for the thousandth time that Michael Hamilton
wasn't quite so heart-stoppingly handsome, that he didn't
look at her with such focused intensity.

'Now, are we both clear on that point, Miss King?'

There was a pause. It lengthened. Amber wished that she
didn't feel so confused; she wanted this job a great deal,
but the thought of actually achieving her aim frightened her
a great deal. Eventually she nodded.

'I work long hours,' he pressed. 'It follows that some of
the time you would have to work long hours too. Are you
absolutely sure that wouldn't be a problem?'

'No.'

'No?'

'I mean yes,' Amber amended hastily. 'I am a career girl,
Mr Hamilton,' she added firmly, 'first and last.'

He nodded approval and glanced down at his desk. 'In your accompanying letter it says you can start work immediately. Is that still the case?'

The hint of possible success was a warm glow inside. Amber damped down the flames of optimism and schooled her expression to be suitably neutral. 'It is.'

'And what about notice to your former employer?' His voice was cool, the stunning eyes watchful. 'You've worked for Miss Brown for several years; how are you dealing with that?'

'I've been a little unwell recently and had to take time off work.' Amber repeated her well-rehearsed line. 'My…employer…is satisfied with my stand-in. She's already indicated there would be no problem about my starting afresh somewhere else.'

'It sounds as if she's happy to be rid of you,' Michael Hamilton drawled.

'Not at all!' Amber pursed her lips in annoyance at the mocking smile, forcing herself to retain her composure; she knew that he was testing her, watching for her reactions. 'But Carol…Miss Brown,' she amended swiftly, 'is a fair as well as an excellent employer and I have some unused leave, so the equation evens itself out.'

'I see. What was the problem?'

Golden eyes narrowed a little. 'Pardon me?'

'You said you'd been unwell. What caused you to have time off work?'

More lies. Amber felt a brief pang of guilt, but pushed it aside before it could take a real hold. This man was a cold-hearted swine—she had to remember that. 'I had a problem with my back,' she improvised swiftly. 'I lifted something heavy and pulled a few muscles. It's sorted itself out now, though.'

'A personal assistant with a recurrent illness isn't going to be a lot of use to me. I need someone I can rely on.'

Another test. Just keep cool, Amber reminded herself; don't take the bait. 'You will be able to rely on me,' she informed him steadily. 'It was never a case of a recurrent illness. I'm completely fit now.'

'I'm glad to hear it.' The far too attractive mouth curved sardonically. There was a slight pause. Strong fingers picked up another piece of paper and Amber caught a glimpse of Carol's familiar advertising-agency slogan. 'I reward work well done,' he continued. 'The salary and fringe benefits more than adequately reflect that fact. But I do not suffer fools gladly. Incompetence, inconsistency, downright dishonesty—all are sackable offences in my eyes.'

'As in mine,' Amber replied with deliberate wintry calm.

'Good. Then we understand one another.' Michael Hamilton rose from his seat. 'You will be informed shortly about the outcome of this interview,' he added brusquely. 'Thank you for attending.' He held out his hand perfunctorily and she felt the scorch of his hand on hers once again.

Amber gazed uncertainly into the lethally attractive face. That was *it*?

'There are no tests?'

He frowned briefly. 'Tests?'

She cursed her own stupidity. What was she doing—making life even more difficult for herself? Did she want this job or not?

Maybe not. It had been easy to be brave in the safety of her ignorance. Now that she had witnessed Michael Hamilton's dangerous, disturbing personality at first hand, she wasn't sure that she would accept the post even if it were offered to her on a platter. Which, after the disastrous beginning, middle and end of the interview, was probably not going to happen anyway.

'Typing, shorthand...' Amber inhaled a breath and tried one last time to look efficient. 'That sort of thing.'

'You stated the level and speed of your typing and short-hand abilities on your application form. Are you telling me I should have reason to disbelieve them, Miss King?'

She shook her bronze head quickly. She had bumped her speeds up, but in essence they had been correct. She could type—sort of. And though her shorthand wasn't exactly the accepted squiggles and scrawls *she* could read it and that was all that mattered.

'No.'

'In that case, I suggest you stop looking so anxious,' he drawled. There was a significant pause. 'After all, what have you possibly got to worry about?'

CHAPTER THREE

AMBER threw down the magazine she had been trying to read in irritation and looked once again at the phone. Four hours had passed since the interview, and every minute had been spent reliving each disastrous and nerve-racking moment of it.

She couldn't stop thinking about him, that was the worst of it. Visually stunning...like a Greek god...simply amazing... The descriptions just flew round and round in her head. Amber leant back in her favourite chair and clutched her head in her hands. She was feeling irritable and edgy and she didn't like it at all. Michael Hamilton had tried to seduce her stepsister, had made life so uncomfortable for Bea when she'd refused that she had had to resign. That was what she had to remember. Just that. Nothing else.

But he possessed charm. She hadn't expected that. He could smile. And when he had done so, it had been wonderful—as if the sun had deigned to shine on an otherwise extremely gloomy day. OK, so underneath it all he was an arrogant swine and would undoubtedly be hell to work for on a day-to-day basis, but the bad vibes she had told herself to expect simply hadn't materialised.

Amber glanced nervously at her wrist-watch for the hundredth time, and then, right on cue, the phone rang.

She jumped as if she had been shot, staring across the room, allowing it to ring for a few seconds, knowing via some sixth sense that it would be his office, and then, with a heart that was pumping fit to burst, she rose and picked up the receiver with shaking hands.

It wasn't his office. It was him. There was no mistaking

30

that deep, precise voice. Her heart, much to her own annoyance, leapt and rolled at the sound of it.

'Miss King? This is Michael Hamilton.'

Who else could it be? she thought. Who else's voice possessed such a sexy roughness even when he was being clipped and efficient?

'The post of personal assistant—are you still interested?'

She inhaled a magnificent breath. Am I? she wondered frantically. Am I *really*? Her earlier act of bravado had been all very well, but the whole afternoon—the unexpected meeting outside the offices, the interview... Deep down it had somehow had a cataclysmic effect. She felt different—jittery, edgy, nervous...excited. Oh, heaven! Amber thought frantically. What will I be letting myself in for?

It was because she had met him. Theory never was the same as practice. Imagining revenge was easy—Amber always had had a brilliant imagination—but doing it...? Actually waging her own private war against someone like Michael Hamilton? Trying to engineer his downfall?

Was she *crazy*?

'Miss King?' He wasn't used to being kept waiting. His voice was clipped and full of authority. He had the sort of cool, arrogant composure that surely only came when you were a multimillionaire and in sole control of your own company.

She swallowed and murmured breathlessly, 'Yes, I'm here.'

'I'm offering you the post of personal assistant. Are you going to accept or not?'

He sounded distinctly impatient now. Amber tried to unscramble her thoughts. After her rather patchy performance at the interview she had honestly believed that she had killed any chance she might have had of getting the job.

Oh, for goodness' sake! What on earth was she hesitating for? So Michael Hamilton had the unfortunate knack of putting the fear of God into a person, and just being in the same room as him turned her legs to jelly! She wasn't going to allow *that* to affect her judgement, was she?

Amber inhaled a sharp breath. 'I accept.'

'Good.' He didn't sound particularly pleased—quite the reverse in fact, as if offering the job to her was something he had been forced into against his better judgement. 'You'll be employed in the first instance on a month's trial,' he informed her brusquely. 'Time enough for me to gauge whether you come up to scratch or not. That's OK with you, I trust?'

'Yes.' Amber kept her voice as level as possible. 'I think so.'

'You'd better *know* so, Miss King. I need firm assurances.

'I accept your conditions, Mr Hamilton,' she replied crisply.

'Good. Eight o'clock on Monday morning, then. I look forward to seeing you.'

Amber held the receiver for a long time after the connection had been severed. The monotonous buzzing was like a warning ringing in her ears. 'He's offered me the job,' she murmured quietly. 'He's actually offered me the job! Who's a clever girl, then?'

Amber replaced the receiver and nibbled nervously on her thumbnail. *Was* she being clever, or just plain stupid?

'Miss King.' Michael Hamilton acknowledged her presence with a nod of his dark head and a gaze that slid over her figure in two seconds and noted every detail of her carefully assembled outfit. 'Not the punctual start I had expected.'

Amber glanced at her watch with a frown. 'I apologise for being three minutes late,' she replied crisply. 'It won't occur again.'

'Pleased to hear it, but you happen to be a little more

than three minutes over time. Thirty would be nearer the mark.'

'Oh, no, I think you're mistaken.' Amber looked at her wrist again. 'It's nearly five past eight.'

'Twenty-five past.' His lips curved, daring her to disagree. 'My watch is never wrong.'

Amber opened her mouth to argue and then shut it again, deciding just in time that discretion was the better part of valour. She felt sure she was right, but there seemed little to gain by proving the point at this juncture.

'In…that case, I apologise,' she murmured, with grudging acquiescence. 'I really had no idea.'

'Oh, come now! It's an old trick. Not one I thought you'd resort to on your first day.' He rose from behind his desk and crossed the room with casual grace.

Amber struggled for all of three seconds—keeping her expression calm and her mouth shut was, she knew from experience, impossible; she just *had* to say something. 'Mr Hamilton, I can assure you that this is a genuine mistake! If it *is* half past eight,' she added stubbornly. 'I have not put my watch back! And I resent the fact that—'

'Coffee?'

Amber, nonplussed for a moment, glanced at the cafetière Michael Hamilton was holding out to her. 'Er… yes…thank you.'

'You look startled,' he drawled. 'Didn't your former employer ever offer you coffee first thing in the morning?' He began pouring steaming liquid into two gold-rimmed coffee-cups. 'And it was meant to be a joke, by the way,' he added, 'about you altering your watch.' He glanced across at her and she knew he had found her prickly response more than a little amusing. 'I thought it might lighten the atmosphere, break the ice, that sort of thing, but clearly it's a little too early in our relationship for humour.'

'Oh.' She felt a complete fool as he handed the coffee to her. 'Well, in that case…'

'You look even more nervous now than at the interview,' he drawled as he retook his seat. 'Anything particular the matter?'

'Well…er…' She struggled to think of something sensible to say, something intelligent. It wasn't easy. Her mind seemed to seize up whenever she was within striking distance of this man and she didn't have a clue why. 'It's…it's just that you look so busy,' Amber finished desperately. 'I feel as if I'm intruding.'

He looked faintly surprised—as well he should, she thought miserably. She was acting and talking like an idiot. She had made another bad start. What was *wrong* with her? Why did she turn into a gibbering idiot whenever she came into contact with this man?

'You've accepted the post as my personal assistant,' he reminded her, with a half-smile. 'The idea, therefore, is that you are meant to assist me. I *want* you to assist me—to *intrude*.' He stared down disdainfully at his desk, which was covered in papers, lifting a hand to smooth back his glossy dark hair which had a rather attractive habit of falling over one eye. 'Far too much paperwork. I feel as if I'm going to drown in it at times.'

He smiled easily, but beneath the healthy tan he looked tired, almost drained. Amber's eyes flicked to the dark jacket which was draped over the back of his chair, to the cuffs of his immaculate white shirt which were turned back to reveal muscular forearms, back to the stunning face which always seemed to draw her attention. It wasn't too difficult to conclude that he had been working for some considerable length of time.

'You've been here since…?'

He glanced up, shifting his concentration from the report he was now holding. 'Since just after six,' he replied. 'I

like to make an early start; there are fewer interruptions.
It's OK,' he added, noting her faint look of horror. 'I don't
expect you to match my hours. Besides—' he threw her an
amused glance '—if this morning is anything to go by, I
guess I'd be asking for the moon anyway.'

'It wouldn't be an impossible request,' Amber replied
stiffly. 'I could do it—if the situation called for it. I mean,'
she added swiftly, realising that she might be talking herself
into goodness knew what, 'if there was something incredibly urgent.'

'That's good to know.' His mouth twitched expressively.
'The next time something *incredibly* urgent comes up, you
can expect to be called out of your bed.' Dark brows rose
and his mouth twitched humorously. 'OK?'

'Fine!' He was making her feel silly—intentionally, she
suspected, although she couldn't be sure. Perhaps he was
like this with everyone.

'Right!' The light, easy expression suddenly disappeared.
'Enough of the banter; let's get to work.'

Amber's heart gave an almighty thud. 'Yes, yes, of
course,' she murmured, attempting a no-nonsense expression, trying to dispel all thoughts of her many inadequacies.
'Where would you like me to start?'

'Firstly, by taking a seat. You look as awkward as hell
standing there. I'll warn you now,' he continued as Amber
perched nervously on the chair in front of his desk, 'because of the sudden departure of your predecessor, there
are quite a few things that have built up in the interim…'

She wondered if she looked as frantic as she felt. The
morning had been hectic enough already. She had lain
awake half the night worrying about everything and anything, and then had slept right through her alarm.

'I doubt if you'll have a moment to breathe, let alone
think about anything else except work for the first few days.
I'll go over a few things with you and then let you find

your own feet. You'll probably have to work late for a few days…'

Damn! She was so nervous that she felt sick, and she had harboured such hopes, too, about appearing cool and calm and collected. Amber took a welcome sip of coffee, relishing the taste and aroma, wishing she had thought more deeply about what she was letting herself in for.

Bea had sounded odd on the phone when Amber had rung to tell her she had got the job. And she had been noncommital and unaccountably edgy when Amber had mentioned the fact that she might need to call on her for the odd bit of help… But she would help, wouldn't she, if Amber got in the most dreadful mess?

'I hope you're prepared for such a commitment?'

There was a pause. Amber registered the silence and realised that Michael Hamilton had asked a question. She placed her cup back into its saucer and glanced up hastily. 'Sorry?'

'Why?' He looked unexpectedly fierce. The words 'granite' and 'steel' sprang instantly to mind. 'Because you haven't listened to a word I've just said, or was the apology for some other reason?'

Amber's 'frantic' level went up another notch. 'No…I have been listening,' she began. 'It's just…'

'Yes?' Michael looked at her enquiringly. 'Miss King,' he continued in clipped tones, when her brain steadfastly refused to come to her aid, 'you don't seem particularly focused. What's the problem?' Dark brows rose imperiously. 'Is it just *too* early in the morning for you?'

He was being sarcastic, but in her panic Amber didn't notice.

'Yes…yes, it is rather,' she replied hurriedly. 'I'm not a particularly early bird, more a night owl—'

'So you don't mind working late?' His mouth firmed ominously. 'Well, that's another bonus! You're prepared to burn *both* ends of the candle—as long as the situation is *incredibly* urgent, of course. Aren't I just the fortunate employer? Well, Miss King, *this* is urgent, right here and now. So if it's not too much to ask, do you think I could have your full and undivided attention?'

He made her blush. She hadn't blushed in years and it felt horrible.

Michael Hamilton began. After five minutes, Amber's head was reeling. She affected a professional pose and tried to look knowledgeable as he proceeded to bombard her— deliberately, she felt—with enough information to fill two notebooks. She longed to ask him to stop, to give her time to digest a few things, to repeat some of it, *all* of it, so that at least fifty per cent of what he was saying sank in, but she didn't.

She just sat there, trying to look clever and competent, even though she knew all the while that she was acting dumb.

'Any questions?'

Amber gulped. She fixed glazed eyes on Michael Hamilton's face and wondered how angry he'd be if she dared ask him to repeat everything all over again. Sense got the better of her. 'No, that's fine!'

She managed a smile of sorts and stood up, desperate to escape so that she could crumble into a heap of incapability.

'Ask Miss Jones if you have any questions about the word processor or the computer. Her office is along the corridor. First on the left. I'm sure she'll be only too happy to help.' He was back to work, dark head bent, elbow on the desktop, one strong hand clenched into a fist, supporting his chin as he read a many-paged report.

Word processor? Computer? Amber frowned in consternation as she began to think seriously of all the gadgets outside this immaculate office which were waiting to contribute to her downfall. Fax machine, photocopier, printer,

Dictaphone... The list was endless. At this moment, even a simple telephone held terror for her.

His calls. What had he said about them? Hold them? Just put through the important ones? How was she supposed to know which they were?

How was she supposed to know *anything*?

The buzz on Amber's desk just over an hour later nearly caused her to fall off her chair in fright. She had been dreading it. That moment when Michael Hamilton would ask for an update on her progress, or want something impossible like the report she was supposed to be finishing.

Amber inhaled a huge, steadying breath, and then scrambled around on her desk, papers falling to the floor as she hurriedly unearthed the intercom.

'Have you got that report finished yet?'

She gulped.

'Amber?'

It was the first time he had called her by her first name, and even with the unnatural distortion of the machine it still somehow managed to sound unexpectedly good.

Honesty, Amber decided quickly, was the best policy. Besides, she thought as she stared at the still unsatisfactory effort in her lap, what else could she say?

'No, not yet.'

'When will you have it ready?'

'Er...soon.'

'OK.' He was giving her the benefit of the doubt; this time tomorrow, she suspected, he would be demanding it on time without any second chances. 'Any calls?'

There had been, masses of them, but Amber hadn't dared to bother him with any of them. 'Just a couple,' she murmured. 'They didn't seem too important; I've noted them down.'

'Fine. I'll take a look later. Have you called my driver yet?'

Amber frowned. She wondered if, after the strain of today, she would have lines permanently etched across her forehead. 'Pardon?'

'My driver.' There was a pause. She heard a distinct intake of breath, then he ordered briskly, 'Come into the office, will you?'

He didn't look particularly pleased. Amber hovered near the doorway to his office and wondered if she should beat a hasty retreat, resign before she made any more blunders. She knew what was coming. She should have checked his engagements, thought ahead, been *efficient*.

'You have a copy of my diary on your desk, do you not?'

'I'm sorry,' Amber replied swiftly. 'I know I should have looked at it, but I got so engrossed in clearing some of the other work—'

He was slipping his jacket on over broad shoulders, hardly listening, or so it seemed to Amber, to what she had to say. 'I employed you to assist me, Amber. Your purpose in life, once you have entered the hallowed portico of this building, is to do anything within your power which will make my life easier, which will relieve me of unnecessary distractions, so that I can concentrate on the smooth running of the corporation.'

He looked at her. Unsmiling. Enigmatic. Amber couldn't tell now whether he was extremely angry, irritated, or just determined to make things as plain as possible from the outset. He clicked his briefcase shut and lifted it from the desk. 'But you should know all this.'

'I do! I do!' Amber raised her shoulders in a gesture of helplessness. She scanned the angular features, recognised impatience in the steely blue eyes and knew it was time to do some grovelling. 'I'm sorry for this poor start,' she

added quickly, managing, with the help of her amateur acting, to sound truly convincing. 'Please believe me when I
say that this really isn't like me. I promise, Mr Hamilton,'
she continued, finding the courage from somewhere to meet
his perceptive gaze, 'that this sort of lapse won't happen
again.'

The pause he left was well timed—his acceptance of her
apology was no foregone conclusion. He confirmed as
much in crisp, no-nonsense tones. 'I don't imagine that I
need to remind you that you are here on a month's trial.
Terminating an employee's contract after less than two
hours would be a little unusual, but not unheard of.' He
surveyed her with a hard expression. 'I need someone I can
rely on, Miss King; surely you can understand that?'

Back to formalities. It was still early days—what was
she talking about? Still early *hours*—but already her prospects weren't looking good.

Amber nodded and bowed her head a little as Michael
Hamilton flicked back his cuff and looked at his watch. 'I
have to leave,' he announced. 'Call the driver now. I'll wait
for him down in the foyer.' He reached the door, opened
it and then turned back. 'And I expect that report you're
working on to be on my desk by the time I return. Is that
clear?'

She managed it, but only just. The rest of her tasks flew
out of the window as she concentrated hard on producing
an immaculate piece of work. With Michael out of the office she found herself able to relax more, and phoning
Beatrice helped—she had been having a great deal of trouble with the printer as well as the computer—and eventually, with step-by-step instructions, she managed to iron the
problems out.

He entered the office when she least expected him.
Amber was wolfing down a cheese and tomato sandwich

as part of a very late lunch, and almost choked herself to death as he entered the smart reception area and strolled over to stand beside her desk.

He looked as immaculate as ever—tall, dark, gorgeously handsome. Hard to believe, Amber reminded herself as she wiped her streaming eyes, that he could have been such an utter swine to Bea...

'Are you OK?'

Amber nodded between vigorous coughing fits. She felt such a fool. *Again.* She tried to turn away, to spare herself the embarrassment of being seen at her worst, with streaming eyes and a beetroot-red face, but there was no escape. A large hand came down and patted her none too gently between the shoulderblades.

'Is that better?'

Amber nodded. She choked and spluttered a few more times, but eventually breathing became possible.

'Well, you don't do anything by halves, do you?' Michael Hamilton sat on the edge of her desk and observed Amber's red face with amusement. 'For a moment there, I thought I'd have to call an ambulance. Here!' He pulled some tissues from a box on top of the desk and handed them to her. 'Wipe your eyes. You look as if you've been crying.'

'Thank you.' Amber dabbed at her eyes, and wondered how much of a mess she looked.

'Your eye make-up hasn't run, if that's what you're worried about,' Michael drawled. 'You still look as beautiful as ever.' His lips curved a little. 'Well, maybe not quite so together.' He glanced at the mess on her desk. 'Looks like you've been working hard. Is the report ready?'

'Yes, it is.' Amber looked up and regarded him with brooding dislike—did he always have to look so together, so sensationally attractive?

'Good.' He didn't whoop or jump with joy at the revelation, as Amber felt like doing; he simply stood up and allowed her the chance to regain her equilibrium by putting a little more space between them. 'I'll look at it in a moment. Are you free this weekend?'

Amber wasn't sure if she had heard correctly, or if he was testing her by having another little joke. She scanned the handsome face one more time and saw that she had, and he wasn't. 'Free?' Anxiety killed the smooth, even tones. 'This weekend?' she continued, aware that every syllable she uttered was higher than the last.

'I have a change of schedule,' he informed her crisply. 'I was due to fly over to Amsterdam next month but circumstances have altered. We need to be there this weekend.'

'*We?* Amsterdam?' Her voice was a positive squeak now. Amber realised belatedly that she was repeating everything he said, too, and added hastily, 'I'm...not sure. I don't—'

'If you have other arrangements, then it would be as well to cancel them,' Michael Hamilton cut in crisply. 'My schedule is extremely tight. I realise this is short notice, but it just cannot be helped. Your passport is up to date, I take it?'

'Y...yes, but—'

'Good.'

'But I...I've only just started working here,' Amber began incredulously. 'You can't be serious!'

'I'm always serious when it comes to business,' Michael assured her. 'This is not an ideal situation, I grant you, but it will help me clarify a certain issue.' He bent and picked up a piece of paper from the floor and held it out to her. 'Do you always work in such mess?'

'What issue?' Amber avoided the last, far too awkward question. Efficiency, as a rule, didn't go hand in hand with

untidiness, and Amber was, amongst other things, re-
nowned for her untidy nature.

'The issue of whether you are competent enough to be
my personal assistant.'

'But you'll be throwing me in at the deep end!' Amber
protested. 'That's not...fair!'

'Fair?' For once Michael Hamilton looked genuinely
perplexed. 'What's ''fair'' got to do with anything? This is
business.' He began strolling towards his office door.
'How's your doggy-paddle, Miss King? Sink or swim. I
wonder which it will be?'

CHAPTER FOUR

FRIDAY evening and Amber was ready, waiting. *On time.*
That was a miracle in itself. The last few days had been
mayhem. Trying to keep her head above water at the office.
Then frantic telephone calls to Carol. A mad try-on of her
clothes. Washing, drying, packing, unpacking, rearranging.
Tears, nerves and nausea. After a pretty disastrous week,
Amber felt totally and absolutely drained.

She hardly cared any more whether the carefully chosen
cream linen trouser suit looked as good as Carol had promised her it did, or whether her hair, which she had tied
loosely at the nape of her neck with a matching cream scarf,
made her look as casually elegant as she had intended.

The gleaming, chauffeur-driven Mercedes drew up outside her north London flat, looking totally incongruous beside the battered jalopies that most people drove in her
district.

Amber dived away from her first-floor vantage point,
picked up her holdall and scampered down the stairs, slam-
ming the front door shut behind her, desperate to shorten
any interested view that her nosy neighbours might have.

She thrust her bag at the chauffeur, who was preparing
to enter the wild front garden, and dived straight into the
back seat of the Mercedes without waiting for any of the
formalities.

'Are you that keen to visit Amsterdam, Miss King, or
just trying to make a quick getaway?'

She thought she had prepared herself—after all, this time
she had known what to expect—but somehow forewarned
hadn't made her forearmed; the rush of adrenalin, the ham-

mering in her chest, the total lack of composure as she sat beside Michael Hamilton in the rear of the expensive silver vehicle told her that.

She didn't have a clue what to say. He looked even more attractive than before, although how that could be she wasn't quite sure. He had changed into a lighter, slightly less formal suit, still smart, with a crisp shirt and tie, but less severe, the paler colours contrasting wonderfully with the sweep of his glossy dark hair and tanned skin. He looked at ease, elegant, in control—the complete opposite of all that she felt.

'Cars like this...' she gestured vaguely at the plush interior '...well...they aren't seen a great deal in my neighbourhood.'

Observant eyes glanced out of the tinted windows and a wry smile lifted the corners of his mouth. 'That I can imagine.'

Amber pursed her lips at his expression. 'Which, roughly translated, means you think it's a scruffy, run-down area!'

'Did I say as much?' Cool eyes rested on her face, challenging her.

'N...no,' Amber admitted reluctantly, 'but—'

'Don't put words into my mouth, Miss King, or even thoughts into my head.' Michael spoke evenly and without edge, but Amber could recognise an order when she was given one. 'I can assure you I'm quite capable and unafraid of speaking my mind.'

Oh, hell! Amber's heart sank. She'd only been in his company for a few moments and already she had had to endure a telling-off. A whole weekend. How would she get through forty-eight hours of being on her best behaviour? She glanced at the uniformed driver, who had taken his seat and was steering the car smoothly away from the kerb. 'Was I supposed to wait for him to open the door or something?'

'Entirely your choice. Bryan won't have taken offence; he's well used to dealing with all kinds of people.'

'Really?' Amber arched her eyebrows and wondered whether she should take offence at this last remark.

'Really.' The attractive mouth curved, and one dark eyebrow rose quizzically. 'Would you like something to drink?'

'What, now? Here?' Amber lifted her shoulders in an awkward shrug. 'Er…yes…please…thank you.'

She watched as Michael opened a discreet cabinet door to reveal cut glass and a choice number of compact bottles. She knew she was acting like a bewildered schoolgirl. She might look the part of a reasonably sophisticated secretary, but that wasn't enough—she had to play the part too.

Michael Hamilton wasn't playing—not at anything. Amber accepted the chilled soft drink he handed her and took a welcome sip. No, she thought, watching surreptitiously as he leant back and stretched his long, muscular legs out in front of him, he didn't have to pretend to be somebody else. Every inch, from the top of his head through his faintly amused expression and right down to the tip of his Italian-made shoes, shouted a man who was in control, at ease with himself and the world around him— even if that world did consist of a crazy, gauche madwoman who long ago—at least seven days ago—had imagined she could engineer some sort of ridiculous revenge.

'I must be mad!' Amber settled herself more comfortably on the leather-clad rear seat, careful to make sure there was a good safe space between them.

'I beg your pardon?'

She paled when she realised she had actually spoken aloud, albeit beneath her breath. Amber glanced across and saw amusement glittering in his mesmeric blue eyes.

She tried to think quickly. 'Er…nothing. Just muttering to myself.' She smiled. 'Bad habit. Must stop it.'

'It could get you into a lot of hot water,' he agreed. 'Speaking your thoughts aloud—it's definitely not what the best personal assistants do.'

'But then you're not sure that I am the best of personal assistants, are you?' Amber replied swiftly. 'It's OK,' she added airily. 'I prefer to get things out in the open. It makes for a better working relationship.'

'Undoubtedly.' His voice held a whisper of sarcasm. 'So you like to be frank. Well, that's good. Presumably you're not averse to others being frank also?'

Amber glanced sideways. 'Of course not,' she replied eventually. 'Why should I be?'

'Because you might not like what you hear, that's why.'

'OK, so I'm having trouble settling in,' she murmured finally, holding herself like an injured soul. 'I admit that.'

'It would be hard to deny it.'

She stung him with a look. 'I'm finding it a little difficult to adjust to working for another person, that's all. I finished that last huge report you wanted in record time.'

'There were a couple of typing errors.'

'Oh, no! Were there?' Amber released a weary sigh. Finding that the one piece of work she had thought she had managed OK was flawed was almost the final straw. 'I'll get better. I'm just…going through a…a rough patch.'

'What sort of rough patch?'

Now what on earth had possessed her to say something so ridiculous as that? 'Don't worry, it's…er…nothing major,' she replied vaguely. 'Or personal,' she added, noticing the beginnings of a frown.

'But I do worry,' Michael replied smoothly. 'Something that affects the efficiency of my personal assistant is a problem that needs to be solved, and quickly. What's the difficulty?'

He wasn't the type of man to tolerate any beating around

the bush; a week of working for him had told Amber that. Much more of her flannel and he would fire her.

'Premenstrual tension.' The idea flew into her head out of nowhere. Amber avoided his gaze and wondered if you could catch a disease called madness. 'I…suffer with it now and then,' she murmured, feeling the heat rising up from her throat. 'It makes all the difference to my performance. It's almost like I'm a changed woman,' she added desperately. 'You know, finding it hard to concentrate, lacking in coordination, scatty…that sort of thing.'

'PMT.' Michael Hamilton said the word slowly. 'Who would have thought it?' His mouth slanted and there was a tinge of irony in his voice as he looked at Amber's flushed face.

'It's no joke!' she replied hotly, glaring at him. 'If you were a woman you'd understand!'

'Oh, I understand the concept well enough and I sympathise. I'm just not so sure about the person it's supposed to have affected. Do you suffer every month?'

'It comes and goes,' she replied airily, wishing with all her heart that she had never thought of something so personal as an excuse, and disconcerted by Michael Hamilton's frank appraisal. Why couldn't he be like every other man she had ever met and go all red and avoid the subject, for goodness' sake? That was what she had intended. 'Do you think we could drop the subject?' she murmured. 'It's a little embarrassing, after all.'

'You brought it up,' Michael drawled. 'Please don't concern yourself on my account, Miss King. Not much fazes me.'

'I wasn't.' Amber turned away and pointedly stared out of the window.

'Irrational, irritable… I hear all manner of personality traits can be connected with it,' he continued coolly. 'Are you sure you feel up to this trip?'

'I'm fine, Mr Hamilton. Absolutely fine.' She formed an expression which she hoped portrayed a woman prepared to endure any amount of discomfort for the sake of her career, and smiled cautiously.

'Don't take me for a fool, Amber.' His tone contained little sympathy. 'It isn't a wise course of action.'

She blushed. 'I...I don't know what you mean—'

'Oh, I think you do.' Michael Hamilton replied. 'Now we're at the airport and we are about to fly to Amsterdam. Let's just forget the past few days and concentrate on the business in hand, shall we?'

That was easier said than done. Particularly with the Mercedes pulling away from the runway and the steps of the Hamilton private jet being pulled into position. Amber felt sick with nerves. She glanced around, expecting him to enter the plane first, but he waited for her to ascend the steps, following close behind, so that she couldn't help but be acutely aware of his presence, of the fact that Michael Hamilton was an intensely attractive, compelling individual.

The interior of the jet was spacious and well designed. Amber hovered, unsure about where to sit. The few seats were arranged around low tables. There was even a small, discreet bar tucked away in one corner.

'Make yourself at home.' Michael indicated an upholstered seat in the company colours of grey and green with a negligent wave of his hand. Amber sat, trying to look composed. 'It's a short flight. Hardly long enough for me to acquaint you with much else except the purpose of our weekend, but that's the way things have turned out. As you said, it will definitely be a case of in at the deep end.'

'I'll cope,' Amber replied evenly, still smarting from his last warning remark. 'I like a challenge.'

'That's just as well, isn't it?' He slipped off his jacket and draped it across an adjoining seat. For a moment

Amber found her eyes drawn irresistibly to the broad, muscular chest, to the place between the buttons of his shirt where the material gaped open a little. She had a brief, tantalising vision of tanned skin and the curl of dark, dark hair...

It shouldn't have happened, Amber didn't *want* it to happen, but the glimpse of his blatantly masculine body played havoc with her body. She felt the stir of sexual attraction deep in the pit of her stomach and hated herself for it.

'He has a company I'm extremely interested in. But he's proving to be a tough nut to crack. He's not keen to sell, despite the fact that his business has been losing money for the past three years.' There was a pause. She registered the silence just in time and averted her gaze from Michael Hamilton's chest. 'So, Amber, tell me...' glinting eyes rested on her face '...how do *you* propose we deal with aged but tough Mr Vincent?'

He had used her first name again. That fact, for a few seconds, mattered more than his question. Then Amber looked up. Did he know she hadn't been paying attention?

She gathered her thoughts quickly. 'Wine and dine him? Convince Mr Vincent that you only have his company's interests at heart?' She hazarded a wild guess and took a gamble. 'It's a family business, isn't it?'

'I didn't say as much, but, yes, it is.' The handsome features relaxed a little and Amber breathed an inward sigh of relief. 'We've met a couple of times before,' Michael Hamilton continued. 'Mr Vincent is very fond of attractive, articulate female company.'

'Meaning?' She raised well-defined eyebrows in puzzled enquiry.

'Meaning I want you to play your part. This meeting hasn't been easy to set up. I don't want things to go awry because you're not well conversant with the complexities of the situation… It would be as well if you fastened your seat belt,' he threw in casually. 'We're about to take off.'

They were indeed. The plane was gathering speed. All at once Amber remembered how much she hated this moment—that awful feeling when your stomach lost all sense of gravity. She hastily grabbed at her belt and fumbled nervously, trying without success to lock the two ends together, hating the sudden sensation of nausea that was settling itself in her stomach.

'Do you want me to do it for you?' She glanced across and saw that he was already halfway out of his seat.

'No…thank you, Mr Hamilton,' she replied swiftly. 'I'm perfectly capable—'

'No, you're not.' He removed the belt from her hands and snapped it together with an efficient click. 'You don't like take-off?'

'No,' she admitted honestly. 'And this one feels worse because it's taken me by surprise.' She gripped the armrests and forced herself to glance around the cabin and talk normally as Michael Hamilton sat in his own seat and fastened himself in. 'If it weren't for the fact that I can look out of the window and see that we're flying…' Amber did just that and then wished she hadn't as she saw the rush of tarmac below. She gulped a breath and averted her gaze. 'This just doesn't *look* like a plane, does it? More like someone's sitting room.'

'You've never been in a private jet before?'

She met his gaze and allowed herself a small smile. 'No.'

Blue eyes rested impassively on her face. 'You look amused—why?'

Amber hesitated. She had allowed the façade to slip a little. Maybe she should have pretended that all this…this outrageous indication of wealth had no effect on her whatsoever. 'I don't come from such an affluent background,' she informed him evenly. 'The chauffeur-driven limousine, the private jet—I can't pretend they don't have an effect.'

The azure eyes were steady and watchful. 'You're impressed by them?'

She frowned. 'I wouldn't say impressed, exactly, but I can't deny it's intriguing to see how the other half live.' She lifted her brows at him in query. 'Have you always been rich?'

It was an impulsive question and one that the sophisticated personal assistant surely would never have asked. Amber regretted it instantly.

Surprisingly he seemed not to mind. He didn't smile, but there was a relaxed, straightforward aspect to his response. 'No. I haven't.'

She decided to pursue it. To her surprise, she found she wanted very much to know things about him—details, bits and pieces of his life. But only, she told herself hurriedly, because it would be useful, for later...when she exacted revenge. 'So, you don't take all this for granted, then?'

'I appreciate the finer things in life, but I certainly don't think they're mine by right if that's what you mean,' he replied coolly.

Had she annoyed him? Amber removed her gaze from his compelling face and thought maybe she had. Too forward as usual, she told herself crossly. When will you ever learn?

They were in the air now. Amber felt immensely glad when the plane finished its ascent and levelled off.

Michael Hamilton was watching her. He made no secret of it. 'I'd like you to call me Michael. Mr Hamilton sounds far too formal when there are just the two of us.'

Her immediate instinct was to say thank you, as if she had been bestowed with some treasured gift, but Amber managed to check herself, merely inclining her head a little. 'As you wish, Mr Hamilton...Michael it will be.' She paused, and added with cool precision, 'You may call me Amber.'

He found her reply amusing, which had not been her intention. She stared, hypnotised, at the flash of even white teeth and told herself that Michael Hamilton knew full well what a potent weapon his smile could be.

He could disarm; Bea hadn't warned her about that. Of course, hard-working, dutiful Beatrice wouldn't have been affected by such blatant sexual magnetism. No, she was far too sensible for that...

Amber shifted in her seat a little and tried not to smile back. That charm, she thought worriedly—it was going to be a hard weapon to defend herself against.

There was no doubt about it—she would have to be on her guard at all times; fraternising with the enemy would see her getting into all sorts of difficulties.

The remainder of the plane journey was spent learning fast. By the end of the flight her brain was spinning with the facts and figures and crisply delivered résumés of business details which Michael Hamilton saw fit to impart.

Was he like this *all* of the time? she wondered. So focused and committed? She wanted to ask him if he had a social life. There had been little evidence of one over the past week. He arrived at the office early and left late. Maybe there was someone who shared his life—a saint who could put up with such a single-minded, business-driven individual. She very much wanted to know. But she didn't ask—even Amber knew when to draw the line.

Amsterdam at night was a sparkling, invigorating place. Ancient buildings lined the streets, glowing in the darkness, their complicated fretwork and ornate spires illuminated. Gleaming waterways reflected the colours of the pretty lights which outlined the many humps of bridges stretching endlessly into the distance.

To Amber, eagerly peering this way and that as a plush limousine whisked them from the airport to their hotel, it felt as if she was visiting a fairy-tale city, not an important commercial centre.

'Here we are.'

She glanced up at the opulent building with its interesting blend of architectural styles and wished that she'd had a little more time to take everything in. After the intense level of concentration needed throughout the week and then the flight, with the added strain of such close and continued proximity to her employer, who at this very moment was placing a firm hand on the small of her back to usher her inside the hotel, she was feeling decidedly shell-shocked.

The formalities were dealt with swiftly and efficiently—Michael was obviously a very welcome guest—and they were escorted up to their rooms. It was another difficult journey for Amber, who had a strong aversion to small spaces of any kind. She managed it, though, keeping her fears battened down whilst the lift whisked them upwards to the correct floor.

'I'll call you up in...' Michael glanced briefly down at his wrist-watch as the hotel porter opened Amber's bedroom door and carried her bags inside '...forty-five minutes.'

Amber frowned. She was still feeling edgy after her few moments in the lift. 'That doesn't give me much time!'

'If you can't take the heat,' Michael drawled, 'you shouldn't have applied to work in the kitchen. Your room is next to mine. Wear something smart and glitzy or you'll feel underdressed—Mr Vincent's girlfriend is quite a dazzler.'

'You make it sound as if I've got to compete with her,' Amber replied frostily. 'I'm your personal assistant, not a geisha girl!'

He looked bored and impatient. 'Just make an effort, OK? I don't expect you to match her head-on; she's the glamorous type. Blonde and tall, with an hourglass figure.'

Amber didn't bother to hide her irritation. She threw him a sarcastic smile. 'With all the sand at the top, I presume?'

He smiled, damn him! He smiled and Amber's stomach flipped a somersault. That made everything worse.

'Something like that,' he drawled. He surveyed her figure without any pretence. Amber knew she looked far from perfect, and it took all of her self-control not to smooth down her crumpled trouser suit and fiddle with her mane of wild hair. 'You look hot and irritated,' he informed her matter-of-factly. 'I trust you'll be up to handling dinner this evening? Three-quarters of an hour,' he reminded her. 'Be ready!'

She wasn't. Not anywhere near. The perfunctory knock on the door exactly forty-five minutes later sent her into a flat spin. Amber cursed, loped across the room unevenly with one foot jammed inside a tight, extremely high black stiletto-heeled shoe and wrenched open the door angrily.

'You're early!' she accused him.

'No, I'm not. I'm on time.' Michael flicked a steely gaze up and down her hastily clad figure. 'Which is more than can be said for you.'

'I just have to add a little jewellery,' she replied swiftly.

'And put on your other shoe,' he added, glancing down at her stockinged foot. 'And fasten your dress up properly.' He walked towards her as she stood in front of a gilt-edged mirror struggling with a dangling earring. 'Here, let me.'

Her heart leapt wildly. There was no way out. Nowhere to go. Michael Hamilton came up behind her and placed his fingers on the zip of her dress before Amber could think of a way to stop him.

'Are you cold? You're shivering.' He knew that she

wasn't. Shocked golden eyes met his steady gaze in the mirror, noted the dangerous charm in the lazy curl of his mouth. 'You look good,' he murmured. 'This dress suits you.'

Amber stared at their joint reflection. If she looked good, he looked stunning. Black and white—a crisp combination. His dark jacket emphasised the broad shoulders; the gleaming white shirt covered a chest that was firm and strong. 'It's borrowed,' she announced baldly. 'From a friend.'

'Good friend,' Michael drawled. 'It looks very expensive.'

It was. Amber was positively terrified of wearing it. It was black and tight-fitting, with a bead-encrusted bodice that Carol had informed her had been sewn painstakingly by hand. Amber despaired at the fact that she might spill something or tear the hem of the flimsy skirt which fell almost to her ankles.

'Are you planning to wear that necklace?' Amber followed Michael's gaze to the top of the dresser and nodded briefly. Another item donated by Carol—the perfect finishing touch to offset the rather daring low neckline of the dress. He reached for it. The sparkling combination of paste and jet looked fragile in his large, tanned hands. Amber watched in horrified fascination as Michael proceeded to lay the necklace around her throat. Every touch of his fingers on her bare neck was like a scorch of fire; every movement, every breath...

'Have you...finished?' Her voice was croaky and she sounded impatient, but she didn't care. She felt a desperate need to put some distance between them before... Before what? Amber glanced at his reflection. She saw no indication in the handsome features of lust or passion or any of the ridiculous things that had dominated her thoughts from the first moment of his touch.

'Good necklace. Is that borrowed too?' His hands rested

on her shoulders. Strong, sexy hands that surely could be infinitely persuasive if they so desired? Beneath the sparkling, low-cut bodice Amber's body burned.

'Y…yes.' She fled from him to the other side of the room and picked up her shoe, jamming it onto her foot without preamble. Then she picked up her beaded evening bag from the bed and marched over to the door. 'I'm ready,' she announced.

He stood looking at her, hands thrust deep into his trouser pockets, making no move towards her despite the fact that the forty-five-minute deadline had surely passed.

Amber glanced across at him, saw the curve of his mouth, looked away and then found her gaze returning to the compelling features. 'Something amuses you?' she enquired stiffly.

The azure eyes held her face. 'Just you.'

'Oh?' She tried hard to look indifferent, casual, even a little bored, but as the curve of Michael Hamilton's mouth widened she knew her attempt at being blasé hadn't come off.

'You're an odd mixture, Amber,' he murmured. 'So cool and controlled one minute, so awkward and embarrassed the next.' He paused a fraction. 'I find that I am, much to my surprise, intrigued.'

Her heart skipped a beat. 'By me?' she replied swiftly. 'What could possibly be intriguing about *me*?'

'Quite a number of things.'

Amber noted the slow, relentless sweep of his gaze, up then down, his stunning blue eyes taking in the swell of her breasts, the curve of her waist and hips, then up again until it was holding her clear oval face. He looked incredibly large and dangerous standing there. The word 'predatory' sprang to mind and her heart missed another beat.

'But this, unfortunately, is not the time or the place to pursue them.' He glanced across at the large double bed in the centre of the room and smiled provocatively. 'Well, maybe the place,' he drawled. 'But the timing is, unfortunately, all wrong.' Laughing eyes surveyed the flush which had appeared on Amber's face for a moment, then he added gravely, 'Lead the way, Miss King. An important dinner engagement awaits.'

The restaurant was swish and exclusive. Amber felt more than a little nervous as they were shown to their table by an efficient-looking waiter.

They were being looked at. Or rather Michael Hamilton was the one drawing the looks—mostly from a selection of well-dressed women at nearby tables. It didn't come as a surprise. He looked magnificent.

Being quite audaciously handsome helped, of course, as did possessing an inherent style, so that clothes that looked ordinary when worn by other men appeared sharper and more distinct on his rugged frame. He wore the understated black suit and the simple white shirt with a dark tie that didn't yell for attention, but it made no difference. Women of all ages looked at him; he looked at them. They glowed when he returned their smiles. You could feel the strength of his personality oozing out from every pore.

He didn't have to say or do anything, just exist—that was enough.

Of course it was just surface appeal, Amber reminded herself as the waiter shook out a napkin and laid it across her lap. She wasn't fool enough to believe that the respect he seemed to inspire in all areas could possibly mean something. So the financial pages talked about him as if he were a god of business; what did that mean?

Amber told herself she'd rather be poor and good than rich and bad any day. She sneaked a look at him from beneath lowered lashes. His whole demeanour annoyed her. Such cool, casual control. What must it feel like to be so successful? Did Michael Hamilton *ever* wake up doubting himself, wondering if he'd made a mistake, regretting things, like other mere mortals? It seemed unlikely.

Amber's blood stirred. She had allowed a lot of important issues to take a back seat. She had been thrown by this sudden change in her surroundings, the novelty of the situation she found herself in. She really wasn't doing herself justice at all. Allowing herself to be disconcerted by Michael Hamilton's actions in the bedroom! Feeling hot and bothered simply because he had zipped up her dress and fastened her necklace and then looked at her as if he'd noticed she was a woman for the first time!

Honestly! What on earth was wrong with her?

The waiter offered Amber a menu and she snatched it angrily from his grasp, her gaze fixed on the man opposite her. Michael Hamilton was a tyrant. Underneath that sharp, glossy exterior was a man with a cruel, ruthless streak. He had ruined Beatrice's prospects of a happy career. She was here for one reason and one reason only. Revenge.

She must remember that. Always.

CHAPTER FIVE

THE food was delicious, the wine list extensive and the atmosphere in the restaurant congenial and surprisingly relaxed.

The impression Michael had given was accurate. Harry Vincent was old but hearty, and his girlfriend was busty and blonde, and extremely beautiful—in an obvious, made-up kind of way.

Amber took a deliberately deferential attitude. She needed to be a success, if only to consolidate her position; one wrong move and Michael Hamilton would get rid of her in a flash—which was what Harry Vincent's girlfriend wanted to do, she thought ruefully as she soaked up yet another hostile gaze.

It was becoming difficult just to sit and take the looks. Amber glanced across at Michael and wondered if he was aware of just how much the woman at his side desired him. It seemed not. The gestures and small flirtatious touches of Harry Vincent's girlfriend had no effect, bouncing off his broad frame, it seemed, like water off a duck's back.

Amber noticed Harry Vincent's irritated gaze. He was no duck and he looked annoyed. She decided he needed a diversion.

'Would you care for a turn on the dance floor, Mr Vincent?' She smiled winningly across at the older man, deliberately ignoring Michael's sharp blue eyes, which missed nothing.

'That would be very pleasant, my dear. Thank you.'

They waltzed to the sound of Mozart on the small rectangular wooden floor—something Amber had never done in her life before. She glanced across after a particularly flamboyant turn and saw that Michael was watching the two of them with open amusement.

'Your employer is an extremely good-looking young man.' Harry Vincent had followed Amber's gaze.

She turned and looked into the lined, craggy face. 'Yes, I suppose he is.'

The old man's smile was knowing. 'You *suppose*?'

'There's more to a man than his looks,' Amber responded evenly.

'Yes, there's wealth and power and sexual charisma,' Harry Vincent replied drily. He eyed the blonde head that was now leaning towards Michael Hamilton. 'Your employer has all those qualities in abundance. It hasn't gone unnoticed.' He looked dejected for a moment, then he twirled Amber away from him with light-footed panache and smiled. 'You're a great little mover. Your employer just doesn't realise what he's missing.'

'Ah, but he does!' The deep, gravelly tones were smooth and good-natured. Michael loomed, large and dangerous, at Harry Vincent's right shoulder. 'May I cut in?'

'There's no need for you to dance with me,' Amber stressed nervously as Michael took her in his arms. 'I only asked him because—'

'I know why you asked him. There's no need to explain. It was a good move.' The dangerous eyes glittered down at her. 'Especially that last one.' His mouth twisted into a smile. 'Harry Vincent seemed to be warming to his task.'

'He needed cheering up!' Amber responded defensively. She glanced up into the strong, handsome face, felt the surge of physical attraction and lowered her dark lashes swiftly. 'I just followed his lead.'

'Well, now you can follow mine.' Michael pulled her closer against his body. His hand at the base of her spine held her firmly, causing a million sensations to shiver up and down her body. 'You did well. Harry Vincent's girl-friend is a man-eater,' he drawled. 'Her attentions were becoming embarrassingly noticeable.' His smile was lazy and full of lethal charm. 'I think it would be as well if we left the two of them in no doubt, don't you?'

Amber glanced up, her brow furrowed into a frown. 'I beg your pardon?'

'At the moment they're under the impression that our relationship is purely that of employer and employee,' Michael explained.

'Well, then their impression would be right,' she replied. 'Because that's exactly what we are!'

'I don't want Harry Vincent backing out of this deal because his girlfriend has got the hots for me,' he replied with unnerving coolness. 'I think it's time we acted like a couple.'

'A couple of what?' Amber retorted sharply.

But she knew. She *knew*.

'There's no need to look quite so aghast, Miss King.' The formal address was like a taunt. 'It won't be that bad, I can assure you.' Michael lowered his head and dropped a sensual kiss onto her mouth. 'Just a little play-acting—that's all I ask.'

Amber stared up into the arrogantly handsome face, her mouth gaping open a little in astonishment. He had kissed her! Damn him! She ran a tongue over her lips self-consciously, narrowing her eyes in anger. Her pulse was thundering like a steam train; every nerve-end in her body felt as if it was on fire. Did the man have no scruples? A stupid question, she told herself swiftly, staring up at the infuriatingly assured features. Of course he didn't.

'We should be dancing.' He began to move her around the floor with unhurried ease. 'After all, that's what we're here for.' He was a good mover, light and easy on his feet, despite the fact that he was six feet plus of finely honed muscle, but Amber hardly noticed.

'You don't seriously expect me to go along with this?' she hissed incredulously.

Harry Vincent and his girlfriend were on the dance floor now, weaving around the other couples, just a few feet away.

Cool blue eyes held her face. 'What do you think?' His hand around hers was warm and strong. He pulled her closer. 'This deal is very important,' Michael informed her quietly. 'I don't want Harry Vincent to get the wrong idea—not even for a moment. Now, smile and relax and try to look as if you want to be with me. They're both looking over.'

She managed the smile, but there was no way she could relax. Not with Michael Hamilton holding her like this. She had never known torture like it. Never. Her body was aware of every movement, every touch. The feel of his hard-muscled body so close to her own left her hot and edgy and totally overwhelmed. She couldn't think of anything except this man, and how it felt to be held within the circle of his arms.

The piece of music finally came to an end. She tried to step away from his hold but he kept her close with casual, deceptive strength. 'Amber, I'm serious about this!' he warned softly. 'Don't let me down. Now I'm going to kiss you again,' he drawled sardonically, with a playful glint in his eyes. 'Only this time I want you to look as if you're enjoying it.'

Amber's heart jolted. 'You can't—!' she began, her golden eyes widening in astonishment, but it was too late.

He could and he did.

It was a longer kiss this time, lingering, full of slow sensuality. The sort of kiss that could leave no one in any doubt. He ranged above her, strong and tanned and full of sexual power, and she was caught, mesmerised by the sexy warmth of his embrace. Lost under the firm, flirtatious mouth—totally, totally lost as a lightning bolt of physical attraction pierced her body. She couldn't move; she couldn't breathe…

Slowly Michael raised his head. 'That's better,' he drawled huskily. 'Even I might be tempted into imagining that you found that enjoyable.'

'In your dreams!' Amber hissed, but she didn't move, she didn't pull away—not even when Michael took her by the hand and led her back to their table.

In his dreams, or in hers? she wondered silently. Hadn't she always longed to be kissed like that?

Harry Vincent's eyes sparkled as they took their seats. 'Well, well!' he said jovially. 'I had no idea! You two seem to have a very good working relationship!'

Michael raised a glass to his lips and took a mouthful of wine. 'Business and pleasure,' he drawled effortlessly, without so much as a glance at Amber. 'Who says the two don't mix?'

The evening broke up some time after midnight. Amber wasn't aware of the exact time. She had lost track of everything as soon as Michael had bestowed his second kiss. It was all she could think about. And the more she thought about it, the more angry she became.

Her farewells were conducted on autopilot. She supposed she smiled and said all the right things, but Harry Vincent and his girlfriend's departure from the restaurant barely registered, because Michael had his arm around her waist. Each finger seemed to scorch through the fabric of her dress. Such a casual, proprietorial gesture, fake and flippant, yet Amber found herself burning with the intensity of it.

'You…you can remove your hand now,' she informed him stiltedly, when his guests were out of sight. 'They're gone.'

'But not for long,' Michael drawled. 'We'll be meeting Harry Vincent again at his office first thing in the morning.'

'Your hand!' Amber repeated with determined coolness. 'If you don't mind.'

He took it away, but slowly, seductively, his fingers dragging across her waist with deliberately slow purpose. 'You sound...indeed you *look* as if you'd like to commit murder.' One tanned finger stroked the edge of her jaw in a deliberately—or so it seemed to Amber—provocative gesture. 'Tell me, do you always react this way when men kiss you?'

'I don't appreciate being used!' Amber replied sharply, jerking away. There was a formidable chill in his eyes. She saw it and quailed. 'You didn't have to...to kiss me... Not like that, anyway,' she added desperately.

'What other way is there?' he replied, with arrogant simplicity. 'Besides,' he continued smoothly, 'our little charade worked. Harry Vincent looked much more at ease by the end of the evening.' His look dared her to disagree. 'Didn't you think so?'

'I suppose he did...yes,' Amber replied reluctantly. She played with a fork on the table, twisting it with a flick of her wrist so that it spun wildly.

A large hand swooped down and covered hers. 'Stop fidgeting!' His voice was sharp. 'And quit looking like a petrified rabbit every time I lay a finger on you!'

'I do not look like a petrified rabbit!' Amber tried to tug her hand away, but Michael Hamilton was exerting too much downward pressure. 'Anyway, what do you expect?' she added heatedly, glaring up into his face. 'What sort of an employer would use such an extreme diversionary tactic just to placate a client?'

'You're telling me you didn't like it?' His smile was one of pure, deliberate arrogance.

Amber felt her face burn. 'Of course I didn't like it!' she lied. 'It was an outrageous thing to do!'

'*Outrageous?* Just one kiss?'

'Two!' Amber corrected him, without thinking.

'Two, then.' His mouth curved with amusement. 'I see you kept count,' he remarked drily. 'Can't have been that bad.'

'It makes no difference whether it was bad or not!' Amber retorted, temper rising. 'You kissed me without permission; that's what I'm objecting to!'

A dark brow was raised in mock query. 'You'd like a formal request?'

'I...er...I...'

Hell! Amber thought miserably. Why couldn't she try being the subservient type and keep silent for a change? Look at the mess she was getting herself into! He had released her now, was taking her by the shoulders, turning her to face him, his hands burning through the beaded fabric of her dress.

'No!' She looked up into the handsome face in astonishment. He wouldn't—would he? 'The staff...the other guests!' She glanced wildly to her left and right, and noticed with a sinking heart that they would be the last to leave the restaurant. There were only a few tired and uninterested waiters clearing tables, and they were over at the other side of the room.

'You'd like us to go somewhere more private?'

'No! No, of course I wouldn't!'

'Here, then.'

Amber caught her breath. For a moment—just for a moment—she wanted to say yes. It was crazy, stupidly crazy, but the moment when his mouth had covered hers, when she had experienced the taste of him, the touch of him...it was a memory that was difficult to dispel. What would a *real* kiss be like? she wondered. A kiss that was full of passion and persuasion...dangerous, dangerous persuasion...

'Amber?'

The sound of her name brought her back to reality with a start. What was she *thinking* about? She looked up and saw that he knew. He *knew*.

She swallowed nervously. 'I'm very tired,' she added, stepping away from him, covering her embarrassment as she fumbled to pick up her bag. 'I want to go to bed.' It just got worse and worse. Her foolish mouth. She blushed furiously, glanced up and saw the amusement in Michael Hamilton's gaze. 'I don't mean—!' she added hurriedly.

'I know.' His expression was pure warmth. 'There's no need to look so apprehensive,' he replied evenly. 'I know what you meant. And I'm sorry. I shouldn't tease. It's not fair. Shall we go?'

He had been teasing? Just that? He hadn't ever *wanted* to kiss her?

Amber glanced at his outstretched arm and walked stiffly past it, aware as she moved down the aisle between the tables of the clipped tread of Michael's footsteps close behind. Aware, too, of the disappointment which coursed through her veins...

The air was cooler outside. Amber inhaled a huge, steadying gulp of oxygen and tried to calm herself. She glanced around as Michael began walking away from the restaurant and frowned. 'Aren't we going to get a taxi?'

He turned and looked back at her, hands thrust deep into his trouser pockets. He was *so* handsome. Every time Amber laid eyes on him—every *single* time—she felt a shock, a thrill of recognition. No matter how hard she tried she didn't seem able to prepare herself for it, for *him*.

Amber clutched her hands into balls at her sides and frowned fiercely. 'I think I'd prefer a taxi,' she murmured.

He strolled the few paces back to the restaurant's entrance where Amber still stubbornly stood. 'I thought you'd appreciate a walk.' He slanted her a look of sardonic amusement. 'It will be a good way of releasing all that pent-up tension you have simmering inside of you.'

'I do not have any tension!' Amber replied tightly. 'Not at all!'

'No?' He considered her tense face without expression. 'Are you absolutely sure about that?'

'I'm tired!' she snapped. 'I've already told you that!'

'I know, but we'll walk anyway.' He didn't seem perturbed or annoyed by her lack of enthusiasm, or indeed her prickly mood. 'The hotel's not far and Amsterdam is very pretty at night. You'll enjoy it.' He tilted her chin with one finger, forcing Amber to look up into his face. 'Trust me.'

Just this—something as insignificant as his finger on her chin—sent her pulses racing, made her heart pound in her chest and her breath come in short, sharp bursts. 'But these shoes...this dress...' Amber glanced down at her outfit, glad of the opportunity of escaping his penetrating gaze.

'They're both perfectly adequate for walking in.' He looked at her patiently and smiled. 'Come on; we both need to loosen up.'

'*You?*' Did he feel the same, then? Amber wondered frantically. Did he feel it too?

'Of course me.' He stopped touching her, flicked back a cuff and glanced at his watch. 'I've been working non-stop for over twenty hours. I need to relax as much as anyone.'

Amber felt a slight twinge of disappointment. 'You work too hard!' she declared.

'Do I?' He smiled. 'Well, then, humour me. Walk with me back to the hotel.'

'I'm not sure you deserve to be humoured.' Amber fell into step beside him as she spoke. They passed a smoky-looking café, still doing business even at this late hour; inside, couples were holding hands over coffee and beer;

outside, groups of young men and women sprawled around the glass-laden tables which were clustered at the water's edge.

'I'm still not forgiven for the kiss, is that it?' There was a telling pause. 'If I told you I've never done anything like that in my life before,' he murmured quietly, 'would you believe me?'

'No.' Amber inhaled a steadying breath. 'Look, can we please just forget it?'

'Do you think that's going to be possible?'

His tone was conversational. Amber looked up at the handsome profile, thrown into dark relief against the glowing lights of the tall, gabled buildings which edged the cobbled street, and wondered frantically if he expected an answer.

It seemed not.

Michael turned to the right and strolled towards the hump of a canal bridge.

'Let's pause here a moment.' He leant on the railing and Amber, after a moment's hesitation, did the same, looking down at the reflection of coloured lights in the oily water below.

'I never thought this city would be like this,' Amber murmured, looking around her. 'It's such a great mix— relaxed and vibrant all at the same time. It's hard to believe that it's a European capital, a hub of the commercial world.' Amber gazed down the length of canal, at the arcs of similarly lit bridges which stretched away in the distance. 'It's very romantic,' she murmured.

'Yes.' Michael's voice was deep and strong. 'Yes, it is.'

'I mean it *could* be!' Amber corrected herself swiftly. 'That's what I meant.' She drew in a steadying breath, closing her eyes briefly in the darkness, cursing the fact that her subconscious thoughts had given her away. 'It could be,' she repeated desperately.

'Would you like it to be?' He turned to face her. Michael's voice was husky. And close. Far too close. He was no fool. She was being as transparent as a sheet of glass.

'I...I was speaking hypothetically! I didn't mean—'

'Are you sure about that?'

'And...and now you're teasing,' Amber challenged. Her voice was sharp and edgy with anxiety. She tried not to remember the taste of his kiss on her mouth, but the memory of it was too powerful. 'You...you said you wouldn't do that!'

'I'm not teasing! That's the last thing I feel like doing, believe me.' She felt the scorch of his touch as he pulled her close. Amber gasped, dismayed and at the same time exhilarated by the feelings of desire which assailed her body. 'Look at me!' Michael commanded, when Amber determinedly avoided his gaze. 'Do you see any sign of hilarity in my expression? Do I *look* as if I'm teasing?'

'N...no.' He was as serious as hell; maybe that was what was affecting her the most—the intensity of the moment...

She shivered uncontrollably and Michael instantly began to remove his jacket.

'You're cold. Here, take this—'

'No!' Amber couldn't bear the tension and strain of being so close to him a moment longer. The warmth of his jacket draped around her bare shoulders was far too intimate, far too enticing. 'I don't want it!'

She turned sharply away from him then, frightened of being too close, of her own mixed-up feelings and the speed at which such feelings seemed to have progressed. Typically, she stumbled on the uneven paving in her borrowed high heels, crying aloud in surprised alarm as the hard, unforgiving ground rushed up to meet her.

'Amber! For goodness' sake!' Michael's hand was sure and firm around her waist. Saving her. 'Are you OK?' He helped her upright, his hands still holding her. 'You know, you're going to do yourself some serious damage spinning around like that.' He smiled gently—*so* gently that Amber's heart skipped a beat. 'This is Amsterdam—remember? And those shoes are definitely not capable of too many high-speed manoeuvres on paving like this.'

'No...' Amber struggled to think of something to say. 'Thank you...for saving me.'

There was a pause, an infinitesimal moment of time, when something shifted, when the world around them both seemed to stand still, holding its breath, waiting...

He was close now, closer than before, closer than was sensible. Their eyes clashed and Amber felt the warmth of his breath on her cheek, smelt the refreshing scent of his cologne, and instantly forgot to worry about the state of her dress, the fact that there had been the sound of fragile material tearing as she fell.

'Is that what I've done?' Michael's voice was low and suddenly husky. 'Saved you?'

'I...I almost fell.'

'You should be more careful.' His eyes burned into her face. Amber felt the scorch of his touch at her waist, burning through the bodice of her dress. She felt hot... weak...confused...astonished that this moment should have flared out of nowhere. That she could *feel* like this.

'I want to get back to the hotel!' It took a tremendous effort of will to drag her eyes from his compelling face, more to force a briskness to her tone and distance herself from him physically by taking a deliberately large step backwards.

He said nothing for a moment, then his mouth curved and his smile was relaxed and understanding. 'If that's what you want.'

'It is.' Amber nodded. 'It's been a long day.'

'Full of surprises.'

'Yes.' She looked at him again. The easy, relaxed smile was still there. It was so simple for him. She must remember that.

Amber was thankful for the cool night air. By the time they reached the entrance to the hotel she felt less heated, not quite so anxious. Unfortunately the brief journey upwards in the lift undid much of her hard fought for composure.

'Don't run away.' Michael had to half run to catch up with her. She had dived out of the lift as soon as the doors had opened onto their floor. He caught hold of her firmly by the arm and turned her around to face him. 'Let's not end the evening like this. You look…' he regarded her pale face closely '…overwrought. Don't be. It was never my intention that I should say or do anything that would upset you. How about a nightcap? It will help relax you.'

He opened the door to his suite, expecting, or so it seemed to Amber, her automatic acquiescence to his invitation.

She lingered awkwardly, watching from the doorway as Michael removed the dark jacket of his dinner suit and tossed it carelessly over the back of a chair. He was being so…nice. There just was no other word for it. Amber bit worriedly down on her bottom lip and wondered what to do.

'You've made it this far,' Michael pointed out as he strolled over to a well-stocked mini-bar. 'Why don't you take a risk and actually come right into the room?' He filled two glasses and then walked to the door and handed Amber a glass of brandy. 'I promise I won't bite.'

His tone was rich with amusement. Amber blushed. She felt ridiculously foolish. 'Don't you think I've got every right to be cautious after the way you treated me this evening?' she replied caustically, taking the glass from his out-stretched hand in a gesture of defiance.

'Back to the kisses, I presume?' His grin was deliberate. 'You really can't get them out of your mind, can you?'

'They infuriated me. You know that.'

'Do I? Are you sure it was fury and not something else?'

Amber pursed her lips and frowned. She couldn't think of a single reply to that. She bent and examined her dress, hoping the flush in her cheeks would subside as quickly as it had arisen.

Her inspection revealed a six-inch tear in the fragile hem. If anything, the damage was worse than she had anticipated. Amber released a small sigh and closed her eyes despondently.

'Stop fretting about it!' Michael's tone was light. 'It's not worth looking so distraught over, surely?'

'Easy for you to say,' Amber murmured. 'Carol will be so disappointed. I promised her faithfully that I'd take the utmost care of it.'

'Why borrow? Haven't you got an evening dress of your own?'

Amber hesitated, then shook her head. 'No. I've never really had the need of one.'

'Not ever? I find that fact hard to believe.' Michael lounged comfortably on the arm of a sofa. 'Surely the advertising agency must have had hundreds of social gatherings to woo clients and generate good publicity?'

She recognised her mistake immediately. 'Er…yes…yes, they did.'

'So what did you do then?' he enquired coolly. 'Wear sackcloth and ashes?'

'No, I wore…' Amber searched her imagination frantically for a suitable reply and found one—just '…dinner suits. Like a man wears,' she added. 'I don't usually go in for glitz and glamour.'

'So I'm honoured, am I?' Michael's gaze lingered on the nipped-in waist and low-cut neckline of the garment she wore. 'How gratifying. Aren't you going to drink that?'

Amber glanced down at the untouched glass in her hand. 'I don't want it. It's too strong.'

'Take a mouthful.' Michael swirled his own balloon glass, warming the brandy in the palm of his hand. 'Like this,' he instructed. 'You'll feel better as soon as it hits your stomach.'

Amber lifted her shoulders helplessly. Never mind the brandy—*he* was too strong for her, that was the trouble. She knew it was pure madness to be here; she felt tired and inadequate, and spending more time than was necessary in Michael Hamilton's company was definitely not the wisest thing to do, but somehow she couldn't find—or didn't want to find—the will-power needed to say no.

'I do feel a little wound up,' she admitted quietly. 'It's been quite a day.' She took a cautious sip. The first mouthful made her gasp, but once it went down and settled inside her she decided it did feel rather good.

'Better?'

Amber released a breath of pure tension and nodded.

'I've really thrown you in at the deep end, haven't I? You've looked kind of shell-shocked all evening. In fact,' Michael added smoothly, 'if I didn't know better, I'd be inclined to think that all this was rather a new experience for you.'

'You would?' Anxiety made her gasp. 'Oh…oh, well, you know…new employer, different circumstances… different ways of working,' she replied quickly.

Michael's mouth twisted attractively. 'You mean your former employer wouldn't have insisted on a kiss?'

'You know full well my former employer was a woman!'

She was lying and it felt awful. Out of nowhere, guilt washed over her. A wave so big that it caused her to frown.

'What's the matter?' Michael asked. 'You look as if someone's just walked over your grave.'

'Nothing!' Amber shook her head and looked away. 'It's probably the brandy.' She swirled her glass nervously. The old adage about two wrongs not making a right sprang into her mind, and she thrust it away impatiently.

'Are you determined to ruin that dress?' The sound of Michael's lazy drawl shook her out of her reverie.

'What?'

'You're slopping brandy all over your outfit.'

'Oh, no!' Amber glanced down at the sparkling black bodice, which was rapidly becoming soaked with alcohol. What was wrong with her? She was acting like an absolute imbecile!

'The bathroom's through there.' Michael gestured with his hand as she glanced around her in panic. 'You'd better douse it quickly, or it will stain.'

He followed her in after a couple of minutes had passed, watching as Amber frantically sloshed water onto the place where the brandy had fallen. 'I came in to see how you were getting on,' he murmured, 'and now I know. Wouldn't it be better to take the dress off?'

Amber kept her head down, pretending to concentrate on her task. 'It's OK,' she mumbled awkwardly. 'I can manage. I'll go to my room.'

Michael leant back against the hand basin, watching in silence. Then without warning he reached forward and removed the towel she was holding and tossed it into the sink.

'What do you think you're doing?'

He showed her. Turning an indignant Amber by the shoulders so that her back was towards him, his fingers took hold of the zip and pulled it firmly downwards. 'You're damaging the material, scrubbing away in that fashion. Don't twist around,' he instructed smoothly as she tried to move. 'What are you acting like some vestal virgin for? You're not naked underneath, are you?'

'N…no.' Amber's reply was breathless. 'But my underwear is…' Her voice trailed away as she searched for a word that didn't sound too provocative.

'Is what?' His voice was light. He was testing her. Teasing her.

Her underwear was black and lacy and only barely decent, but she had no intention of telling him that. The zip had reached the base of her spine. An uncontrollable shiver racked Amber's body.

'You can't be cold,' Michael drawled. 'If anything, it's far too stuffy in here.'

'Stop it! This isn't fair!' Amber decided that attack was the best form of defence and twisted around, crossing her hands over her breasts, holding the dress against her to prevent Michael Hamilton from seeing anything more than he should. 'Don't look at me like that!' She frowned. 'You may think it's amusing but I don't!'

'Amusement was the last thing on my mind,' Michael replied quietly. His gaze fell to her body. There was a dangerous pause. 'Stupid move,' he murmured quietly. 'I wasn't thinking. Better, maybe, to let you ruin the precious dress rather than…'

He didn't finish. The moment outside the hotel repeated itself, only this time the situation was far more hazardous, balanced on a knife edge.

They looked at one another in silence for what seemed like eternity.

'*Please*…' Amber's voice held a note of desperation as she surveyed the man opposite her in wide-eyed dismay. 'Michael—'

He wasn't listening—or if he was he didn't care. 'Sorry if this upsets you,' he murmured huskily. 'But, you know, some things are just meant to happen.'

They were. She knew it. A fierce, sweet ache ran through her body, and that was even before he kissed her.

Maybe anticipation was everything, Amber thought, and then Michael's mouth covered hers and she knew that it was barely a fraction of total enjoyment, as his lips moved with seductive assurance over her partly opened mouth, as the kiss lengthened and grew in intensity, as his hands moved up and cupped her face, caressing her skin, sending shivers of awareness through the whole of her slender body.

The evening gown slipped forward and she felt the electricity of shock as strong fingers slipped beneath the black lacy straps, dragging them over her shoulders, down along the length of her arms. His kiss was full of silent passion. His hands skimmed across the soft mounds of her breasts, skilfully began to explore the flat planes of her stomach, to edge sensually towards the edge of her briefs...

'No!' Amber's gasp echoed noisily in the small space. She drew back sharply, pressing her body against the hand basin in an effort to put space between herself and Michael. 'No!' she repeated shakily. 'You...you can't do this!' She was breathing hard, far too hard. She closed her eyes for a moment, struggling to regain her composure. 'This shouldn't be happening!'

'Why not?' The blue eyes that met hers were genuinely questioning. She saw in amazement that Michael was totally unrepentant, unmoved by her outburst. 'Why shouldn't it?'

Amber clutched her dress against her burning body like a shield and shook her head wildly. 'Because...it just wouldn't be right, that's all!' She didn't know what to say. What *could* she say? That deep down she *had*, despite everything, wanted things to go further?

'Not right?' Smouldering eyes met hers. 'Explain.'

'I don't have to!' Amber tried to move, but the bathroom

was small and Michael was blocking her path. 'Why should I?'

'You imagine I seduce all my personal assistants—is that it?' he asked. 'Well?' he added sharply, when she made no reply.

Golden eyes narrowed. Amber worked hard to collect the required hate she needed to deal with the situation and found a great deal of it lacking. 'Don't you?' she whispered, thinking finally of Beatrice.

He smiled. A slow curving of his lips which sent shivers of awareness up and down her half-dressed body. 'No,' he murmured. 'As a matter of fact I don't. But that doesn't mean there can't be a first time for everything, does it?'

'Not with me!' He was lying—he had to be. Easy conquests—that was what it was all about. Well, Beatrice hadn't been one and neither would she be. Amber tried to move past him, but Michael sidestepped neatly and blocked her way again. 'I want to get out of here!' she gritted.

'You're turning what just happened between us into something distasteful,' Michael ground out. 'Why? We know—we *both* know—that—'

'No!' Amber pressed her hands to her ears. She wouldn't hear it. She wouldn't let him charm her with his smooth patter. Maybe he had said all this to Beatrice; maybe she should have asked her sister for all the sordid details so that she could have been better armed against the repeat performance.

She glared at him in the small confines of the bathroom. The heat in the pit of her stomach was almost too much to bear. Michael Hamilton's presence was totally overwhelming. Amber had never known such intense physical attraction as this. She didn't know what to do, how to handle it.

'Your eyes have a hypnotic quality.' Michael's voice when he spoke was unexpectedly slow and deep and husky. 'Gold and green,' he murmured. 'Full of the most delicious temptation. *Are* you tempting me, Amber?' he asked, almost conversationally. 'Is that haunted, virginal look planned for effect? Because if it is—'

'No!' She stared into the handsome face, aghast. 'No,' she repeated, shaking her head. She looked at him, trying to deny the way she felt, the way he made her feel. 'I have to get to my room!' she blurted out wildly. 'Let me pass!'

He moved then.

She knew he watched her as she fled from the bathroom.

What was he thinking? she wondered. Did he really believe that deep down she wanted him? And didn't she? Hadn't she felt the most compelling desire to give in, to allow his hands and his mouth to continue their work of seduction? Oh, hell! she cried silently. What on earth have I got myself into?

Amber found her bag on the sofa and bent to pick it up. She looked down at her hands, which were trembling violently, in something approaching despair.

She had wanted him. She had wanted him so much...

'Use this.' She jerked upright as Michael walked across the room and opened the connecting door between the two suites. 'It will be more convenient.'

For what? Amber wanted to know. For what?

'I'll see you in the morning.' Michael touched her shoulder as she passed and she felt the scorch of his fingers on her bare skin. She turned sharply as if she had been burnt. Compelling blue eyes scanned her face. 'I'll meet you at eight for breakfast in the dining room.' His eyes held hers for a long moment. 'Are you...all right?'

Amber nodded, murmured an incoherent reply and then walked through the doorway into her own room. After a moment's hesitation she turned and glanced back. But Michael Hamilton wasn't there. All she saw was the glossy whiteness of a firmly closed door.

CHAPTER SIX

THE night had seemed endless. Amber had managed little sleep, and when the bliss of unconsciousness had been obtained she had found herself beset by strange dreams and unvoiced anxieties.

She wondered if it was worth the struggle to try and improve her look. Her face was too pale this morning, dark shadows beneath her eyes revealing her pitiful lack of sleep.

She picked up the sage-green linen jacket from the bed and slipped it on. At least the outfit she had chosen to wear fitted the part of an efficient PA even if she didn't. The muted colour suited her, she decided; so did the matching skirt. She smoothed it down over her hips and wondered if it was just a shade too short. No, she was being hypercritical. It looked fine and her hair had worked well too.

She checked the tightly coiled rope of gleaming bronze fastened with a discreet clip at the nape of her neck. Not bad, she told herself; at least it was a contrast to the confused, dishevelled image she'd presented last night. Maybe Michael Hamilton would have forgotten all about that by now...

A few minutes later Amber scanned the dining room quickly and spotted him sitting at a table in front of one of the elegantly draped windows which looked out onto a quiet, tree-lined courtyard.

She hesitated a moment, finding the resolve from somewhere to cope with the memories of last night, then approached with measured steps.

He was reading the morning paper, his dark head lowered, his eyes scanning the indigestible financial news of the day with intent regard. Eventually he became aware of her presence. He looked over the parapet of paper, holding Amber's face for an infinitesimal measure of time.

'Good morning.'

Her reply was barely audible. She sat opposite, fiddled with her napkin, glanced out of the window, checked the contents of her bag. Then she looked around the room at the other diners.

'Why don't you pour yourself some juice?' Michael suggested smoothly. 'Breakfast will be here in a moment.'

'I'm not sure that I'm particularly hungry.' Her voice was ridiculously haughty. She hadn't meant it to sound like that. 'What do you expect me to do this morning?'

He didn't like her tone. Deep down she couldn't blame him. The newspaper was folded and placed to one side. 'Pay attention. Take notes.' His voice was crisp. 'It's just an informal visit. If all goes well we'll start proper negotiations for the takeover shortly.' He scanned her face with enigmatic eyes. 'Did you familiarise yourself with the reports I gave you?'

'Yes.' She had spent hours going over them. Hardly the stuff to help sleep, but it had been better than staring into the dark thinking about him.

'And what conclusions did you come to?'

'Me?' Amber frowned. She might have read them, but she hadn't known she was expected to come to conclusions. 'Well...I...' His hair was damp. A disconcerting picture of him standing naked under the shower flashed, unasked, into her mind.

'You did reach an opinion, I take it?'

His gaze was daunting. Amber thrust the powerful image that had sprung out of nowhere away and forced herself to concentrate. 'Well...it seems to me that Vincent Construction is vastly overmanned,' she murmured, fran-

tically trying to remember some of what she had read in
the small hours. 'He's had a drop in orders and—'

'And he should have laid half the workforce off months
ago,' Michael finished for her. Amber nodded reluctantly.
'That's what you think?' he queried, raising a dark brow.
For the first time that morning he looked half-interested.
He poured coffee into two large, round cups and pushed
one of them across the table towards her.

'Yes.' She hesitated, and then, encouraged by his response, added more boldly, 'I can understand why he hasn't
done anything about it, though. From what I could gather
last night, his workforce are a loyal bunch. A great pro-
portion of them have been with him a long while. He
doesn't want to lose them.'

'Every one of them will be looking for work, if he
doesn't sort the company out soon,' Michael replied tersely.
'He should realise that. The trouble is, he doesn't want to
face facts.'

'What will you do,' Amber asked, 'if you buy the company?'

'*When* not if,' Michael corrected her crisply.

A waiter approached with a trolley full of food. Dome-
shaped lids were lifted to reveal steaming mounds of crisp
bacon and scrambled eggs. Amber glanced over appreci-
atively as the waiter began serving breakfast and decided
she was hungry after all.

'You seem very sure of the outcome. Do you always get
what you want?' she asked, with undisguised interest.

Searing blue eyes held hers, reminding her of the force
of his personality, of what had taken place between them
the night before. 'Yes.'

Amber swallowed. She was playing a dangerous game
and the stakes were high. In that moment she felt something
akin to fear. But fear for her sanity, not for her safety.
'Lucky for you!' she answered with forced flippancy.

'Luck has nothing to do with it.'

Those eyes! Amber glanced quickly down at the plate of food in front of her and inhaled a surreptitious breath. She picked up her knife and fork and worked hard at regaining what little she had left of her composure. 'Vincent's company,' she croaked, after a long pause. 'What do you propose to do with it?'

'I'll slim it down and split it into smaller components.' Michael picked up his coffee-cup and drank a mouthful before continuing. 'The whole operation is far too unwieldy. It's got away from him. He knows that—he's not stupid—although I doubt he'd ever admit it. Harry Vincent has expanded in all the wrong areas and he's lost control. And when you lose control,' Michael delivered firmly, 'you lose advantage.'

Amber paused with her fork halfway to her mouth. Losing control was something Michael Hamilton had probably never done in his life. Listening to him now, remembering his coolness of last night, she understood why that came as no big surprise. 'You'll break it up?' she queried, frowning.

'That's right.'

'Harry Vincent won't like that.'

'It won't be any of his business. He'll have sold it to me before then and the problem will be out of his hands.'

Amber hung her head and concentrated on her food for a moment. 'I don't understand why you want this company,' she murmured. 'What's in it for you?'

He looked across. His dark brows rose in surprise. 'Profit, of course. What else?'

Amber shook her head. 'But how? I don't understand—'

'Nor do you need to,' Michael responded bluntly. 'Now eat up. I want to be punctual. We have to cross to the other side of the city and the traffic's going to be busy.'

*   *   *

They arrived at Vincent Construction spot on time and soon found Harry Vincent's office.

The old man didn't look particularly pleased to see them, Amber thought. His face was drawn and pale, and when he greeted them he sounded dreadfully out of breath.

Amber glanced across at Michael to see if he had noticed the change in the man who had been their jovial companion the night before. It seemed he had—that and more besides.

'Mr Vincent?' Michael rounded the desk and placed a hand on the man's shoulder. 'Is there something I can get you? You don't look particularly well.'

'Young man, I'm fine!' His reply was irritable. Craggy, impatient fingers brushed Michael's hand from his shoulder. 'Overindulged myself last night, that's all.' A wrinkled hand hovered near to his chest. 'Now let's get on with the business in hand, shall we? I thought we'd start with a look around the workshops...'

The tour was endless and, to Amber at least, incredibly boring—lots of noise and grease which made her fear for her hearing and the safety of Carol's sage-green suit. Eventually they made it back to the office.

'Could your secretary take notes?' Harry Vincent enquired gruffly as they took their seats around a gleaming conference table. 'Mine doesn't come in on a Saturday.'

Michael nodded. 'Certainly.' He glanced in Amber's direction. 'Have you a notebook?'

'Of course.' Amber tried to keep her panic under control as she delved in her handbag for pencil and paper. Strain clenched her features. Was there a possibility that the two men would speak slowly and in words of only one syllable?

Not a chance. They talked informally but at great length and speed about the proposed takeover, often using words that Amber had no idea how to spell, let alone jot down in shorthand.

She began to feel desperate. She knew she would never

be able to decipher anything. 'Just the salient points,' Michael had murmured before they'd started, possibly recognising a little of the anxiety on Amber's face. She looked despairingly down at the notebook covered with squiggles and scrawls, which rested out of sight on her knee, and doubted her ability to decipher *any* point, let alone a salient one.

'Right! I think we've covered most things.' Harry Vincent rose from his chair and strolled to the window which overlooked a vast car park. 'I think it would be a good idea if we could hear the main points of our discussion.' He turned briefly towards Amber. 'Miss King, if you please...'

That awful sinking feeling—she hated it. Heat engulfed Amber's body as she shifted awkwardly in her seat.

Michael frowned. 'Amber, are you ready?'

She glanced down at her notebook, rifling back through the pages until she found the beginning. She stared hard, willing herself to remember, but soon the squiggles were misted by tears and it took a great effort not to allow the sob which was caught in her throat to escape into the room.

'Miss King, if you could hurry along,' Harry Vincent snapped irritably. 'My time, like that of your employer, is precious!'

'What's the matter?' Michael's voice was low.

'Nothing.' Amber stood up. Drastic action was the only thing that would save her. 'I just feel a little faint, that's all. It must be the heat and noise of the factory floor, and it is rather stuffy in here.' She leant forward, resting her hands on the polished table, and knocked her half-filled cup of lukewarm coffee all over the cause of her problems— the notebook.

'Oh, I'm terribly sorry!' Relief flooded through her as she saw how badly the pages of notes were soaked. 'I'm *so* clumsy! Please forgive me.'

She began to mop ineffectually with a tissue, until Michael reached forward and placed a restraining hand on her arm. 'Leave it!' he commanded. 'Now!'

'Oh, for goodness' sake!' Harry Vincent turned abruptly from his position at the window and strode towards Michael. 'We'll talk again—maybe,' he announced gruffly. Amber glanced up. Beneath his expression of irritation his face looked pale and lifeless. 'I need time to digest the proposition you have put to me.'

Michael rose and held out his hand. 'I look forward to it.' He scanned the older man's grey face and added, after an infinitesimal pause, 'It's been a tiring morning. Maybe we're all a little under the weather after the revelry of last night.'

'Yes...yes, you're probably right.' For a moment the mask that Harry Vincent had fixed in place dissolved to leave a very tired, frail-looking old man. 'I think I'll go home and take a rest; I'll leave you both here if I may.'

The conference door closed.

'Do you have to be *quite* so clumsy?'

Amber bit down on her bottom lip. She felt nervous. Michael's voice was calm—a little *too* calm, perhaps? 'I really am very sorry,' she murmured.

'Yes, so you keep saying.' He reached forward and picked up the sodden notebook. 'What a pity these are no use, and after all your hard work, too,' he added sarcastically. 'I suggest you drop them straight into that bin over there.'

'Mr Vincent wasn't very pleased, was he?' Amber muttered miserably.

'Did you honestly expect him to be?' Michael's voice was sharp. 'Incompetence isn't something any employer likes.'

'It's just...well...he was so jovial last night, so easy-going—'

'And you thought he'd take that little charade with the coffee in his stride?' Forceful blue eyes held her face. 'Pretty drastic action, wasn't it?'

Amber tried to look puzzled. 'I don't know what you mean—'

'We could always dry out the pages. You didn't use ink. A great deal of it should still be decipherable—or not, as the case may be,' he added pointedly.

'OK! OK! So my shorthand's a bit rusty.'

'It's practically non-existent, isn't it?'

'I…I got flustered. I have my own system—a combination of shorthand and speed writing—and…well…I got into a muddle early on and…I just didn't seem to be able to think straight.'

'So, your CV—that was a lie, was it?' Michael's look was uncompromising. 'Anything else I should know about? You *can* type and use a word processor, I presume?'

'Yes, yes, of course I can!' Amber frowned in consternation. She felt awful. Should she come clean—admit to everything, to the whole stupid lie? The way ahead spelt madness, she knew that, but something—or rather some-one—was holding her fast. The space around Michael Hamilton was like one vast magnetic field; the closer you got, the bigger the pull. 'I'm sorry I ruined the meeting,' she murmured. 'I really upset him, didn't I?'

'Harry Vincent seemed pretty upset before,' Michael replied tersely. 'I don't think it's necessary that you should shoulder the blame entirely.' He picked up his briefcase from the floor. 'OK, you can stop looking so petrified. I'm not going to roar and breathe fire.'

'Why not?' She almost wanted him to rant and rage. She felt bad about the way she had acted—inadequate, deceitful, guilty… The list just went on and on.

'Maybe it's because I'm a nice, even-tempered sort of

guy,' Michael replied wryly. He threw Amber a sharp look. 'Ever considered that?'

On their way back to the centre of Amsterdam they heard.

She sensed that it was bad news almost before Michael had put away his mobile phone and turned with a grave expression to look at her. 'Harry Vincent has had a heart attack.'

'No!' Amber's hands flew to her mouth; her golden eyes were wide with horror. She took a deep breath. 'Is he…?'

'He's alive, but it *is* serious.'

Amber turned and looked out of the window at the crowded streets teeming with life. 'It's my fault,' she murmured tremulously. 'If I had been more efficient—'

'You can't honestly believe that would have made any difference. Amber?' She felt the strength of Michael's hand on her arm, relentlessly turning her to face him. 'Harry Vincent was…is ill. It has nothing to do with your—'

'My ineptitude! Say it, I don't mind. It's the truth!' She shook her head wildly. 'I always, always make a mess of everything!'

'No, you don't.' Michael's voice was soothing, kind. It made Amber feel worse, made her feel even more like castigating herself.

She tried to look away as a mist of tears veiled her eyes, but determined fingers reached up and held her face. 'It's not as simple as that,' Michael asserted. 'You saw as well as I did how changed he was.'

'OK, so he must have been ill before,' she admitted slowly. 'But I brought it on. He was angry. He practically stormed off. I raised his blood pressure, if nothing else…' Amber frowned. 'Oh, I hate myself for making such a mess of things. I ruined the meeting, and you…' She swallowed back the lump that seemed to be stuck in her throat and slanted Michael a miserable glance. 'You had worked so hard to set everything up.'

'Now you're concerned about my welfare?' His features showed amused benevolence. 'Hell, Amber, you really do want to shoulder all the blame, don't you?' His eyes held hers for a long moment. 'Why is that?'

She didn't reply. She felt so confused. So miserable. How could she tell this man that she longed to be held, to be touched, to be comforted and told that everything was going to be all right? How could she? He probably longed to escape. She was everything he hadn't expected. He had hoped for a strong, straightforward woman who could cope with most if not all eventualities. A professional. And what had he got?

What, indeed? Amber didn't want to make herself even more upset by dwelling on her failings.

'Come on. Let's get some fresh air.' Michael leant forward, murmured something to the driver and soon the car was pulling to a smooth halt. The door was opened and he reached out a hand. 'We'll walk.'

'Where?' Amber felt his strong fingers, firm and warm against her own, and found that she felt more fragile than she ever could have anticipated.

'Anywhere.' Michael's gaze was searching as he looked into her face. 'Does it matter?'

It was a wonderfully sunny day, and the people of Amsterdam—residents and tourists alike—were making the most of the pleasant weather. It was good to walk along the canal banks, beneath the dappled shade of many hundreds of trees, to feel the warmth of the day permeating her young body. Original, brightly painted barges chugged up and down the canal, sandwiched between open-topped motor launches crammed with visitors.

But Amber, head down, scarcely noticed. She placed one

foot in front of another and tried to fix her thoughts into some kind of order.

'You know, going over and over it in your mind won't solve anything. In fact it may well get you killed,' Michael told her, his voice rising in concern as Amber walked dangerously close to the edge of the canal.

He tugged her close suddenly, turning her in the middle of the path to face him, scanning her preoccupied expression with open curiosity. 'Now look at me!' he commanded. 'I want to know about you. I want to know what's going on in that beautiful head of yours.'

It was a shock, hearing him call her beautiful. Not that it *meant* anything, of course; it was just a flip comment, something to make her feel better. He didn't look flip, though, Amber realised with a jolt as she gazed into Michael's handsome face. Not at all...

'Why exactly are you torturing yourself like this?'

She shook her head, frowning a little. 'I can't explain.'

'Can't or won't?'

He was close—*very* close; she could feel the brush of his thigh against her own, the sweep of his arm around her waist, the scorch of his hands against the small of her back. It was affecting her judgement. His mesmeric blue eyes were focusing on her with such intensity that a great part of Amber actually believed it would be a good idea to unburden herself.

To trust him. Now that would be a wonderful thing. To tell him everything...

Ten years ago... That was where her thoughts had raced to after hearing the news of Harry Vincent's collapse.

Amsterdam—sunny and vibrant, full of tourists and residents, a glorious, bustling city with the sun glinting on the surface of the canals which were the focus of the city, bikes and cars and boats. For a moment she wasn't there. Ten years ago—that was all she could see. That moment when her life had been changed utterly, irrevocably.

A motor launch passed by, filled with camera-clicking tourists. The horn blared and Amber jumped as if she had been shot.

'Hey, calm down.' Michael's arms tightened reassuringly around her body. 'We can't talk here,' he murmured. 'I understand.' There was a pause, and then he added with a somewhat forbidding amount of determination, 'We'll find somewhere else.'

He led the way down a narrow side street. There was a gate at the end and they went through it.

'This is the Begijnhof,' Michael told her. 'Quiet enough for you?'

'It's...enchanting!' Amber replied simply, looking around in wonder. 'The houses are so...so perfect.'

In an instant it was as if they had been transported back to the Middle Ages. They were in an old square with iron railings and gardens and houses surrounding a small church with a slender steeple. Amber looked around her, amazed by the silence. It was hard to believe that the hustle and bustle of the main centre was only metres away.

'The oldest place is some five hundred years old.' Michael took Amber by the arm and pointed up at the gables of the buildings closest to them. It was difficult to concentrate on his words. Too many distractions. Too much awareness of his body and the strength of the man. 'See the stone pictures of biblical scenes?' he murmured. 'They were used in the olden days to distinguish one residence from another.'

Amber examined the houses with a particularly close scrutiny. Playing for time. Wondering how she was ever going to unburden herself to a man whom she had counted as an enemy only a few days ago.

'So tell me...' Michael's gaze was direct and uncompromising. 'What happened?'

'Sorry?'

Michael's look revealed all. Feigned puzzlement wasn't going to get her anywhere. He didn't say anything; he didn't have to. Don't play games. Don't waste my time. It was all there in his eyes and the slight curve of his mouth.

'It was a long time ago.' Amber moved restlessly, running her hands along the iron railings, still looking up at the miniature houses, still trying to act her way out of the incredibly uncomfortable position she found herself in.

'You haven't forgotten.' It was a statement, not a question.

'No.' She paused, caught by his forceful gaze. Silly, really. If she was matter-of-fact about the whole experience, told him straight in as few sentences as possible, the confession would be over before she realised. 'When I was twelve...' Amber swallowed and then inhaled a steadying breath '...I came home from school one afternoon. My father was a writer.' She managed a smile. 'Children's books. Great fun. He had made some tea. We always shared a cup together. There were my favourite biscuits on a plate—chocolate bourbons...' She paused and gathered her resources. The sun was pleasant on her face, and there was a cooling breeze, but she felt hot and curiously light-headed. She brushed a heavy strand of hair from her face and forced herself to go on. 'Sorry. I'm not making much sense.'

'You're doing fine.'

His voice was softer than she'd expected, almost sympathetic. Somehow it made things worse. Her pulse was beating far too quickly. Amber turned abruptly and continued walking. Her smart shoes sounded crisp and efficient on the paved walkway; beside her Michael adjusted his long stride to suit her slower pace.

'I kissed him hello as usual,' she continued stiltedly, 'and he smiled and lifted the tray to take it through to the conservatory and then…then he fell to the floor…' She faltered into silence. It had happened over ten years ago, but the pain still wouldn't go away, nor the feeling of panic. Amber relived the scene in her mind—flashes of torment and hysteria and black, disbelieving grief.

Tears welled up in her eyes and spilled onto her cheeks. She walked faster so that Michael wouldn't notice, wanting to run from him but finding her legs were too shaky and feeble.

'Amber!' He caught her by the arm and turned her relentlessly to face him. 'I'm sorry.'

Her breath caught on a sob. She forgot to care about whether Michael Hamilton saw her crying. 'He died, right there in front of me,' she croaked, 'and I didn't know what to do. I watched his life ebb away. I was so…so *useless*!'

'You're being too hard on yourself. You were just a child.'

Tormented eyes scorched Michael's face. 'But he died and I didn't do anything to help him!'

He pulled her close then, when Amber's misery was at its peak, holding her tightly, wrapping his arms around her slender body, rocking her as if she were a baby. 'Don't torture yourself like this.' His words were soft against her hair. 'You have nothing to blame yourself for. And you can't change the past.' Michael's voice was deep and urgently husky. 'It's over. Gone.'

'But I miss him so!' Amber lifted her head from his chest. She felt the warmth of his hand against her cheek as he wiped away the tears with infinite gentleness.

'I understand.' She looked up into his face and found that she believed him implicitly. Why? she thought. And why does it feel right to be held like this, by this man?

She didn't imagine that he would take advantage, not

there and then, but he did. Or was it a mutual thing? How much had Amber instigated the passionate kiss which took her breath away and forced all the feeling that had been simmering below the surface to surge and flame into dramatic life?

His mouth was a revelation, strong and sure, moving with wanton licence over her softly parted lips. She clung to him, feeling his strength beneath the fabric of his jacket. Dazed by the overwhelming feelings of passion and need that his kiss produced. Deep inside she wanted him to do everything. To take all that she could give and demand more and more.

Images flashed into her mind. Treacherous thoughts that left her weak with need. All or nothing, Amber told herself. This man wouldn't do anything by half measures. He would be the most passionate of lovers or he would be no lover at all.

She could barely understand it. How could this man, this individual, whom she knew to be cold-hearted and ruthless, do this to her?

He broke their embrace, and as soon as it happened it was as if a light had gone out somewhere in Amber's life.

Adrenalin was high, pumping through her veins, and she was panting, her breath coming in short, uneven bursts. It hadn't been enough. It should never have happened in the first place, but that didn't alter the fact that now she had tasted the beginning she desperately desired the end.

They looked at one another. Neither spoke. Silence engulfed them as they stood in the sunshine before the quaint houses and sleepy church.

Amber couldn't think straight; looking up at Michael Hamilton made her wonder if he could either. Being cold and calculated hadn't come into it. What they had just experienced had been passion of the purest kind, and it was a shocking thing to have to handle after the upset of the morning and the angst of her confession.

She took the easy way out and ran from him, from what had just taken place between them. Her surroundings were a blur as she headed for the gate which led into the narrow side street, tears streaming down her face. She would head back to the hotel. She would pack and wait for him, and when they were back on safer territory in England she would decide what she should do.

Thoughts chased through her mind as she ran, mocking her, taunting her. Where was her anger now? Where was the all-enveloping feeling of revenge that had brought her this far? She was supposed to hate Michael Hamilton, not feel like *this*!

He caught up with her in the narrow side street. The time for compassion had passed. Angrily he spun her around and backed her up against a rough stone wall. 'Where on earth do you think you're going?'

'Back to the hotel.' Her voice was weak and ineffectual. 'To pack.'

'Why?'

Amber found the courage and looked him straight in the face. 'I can't sleep with you.'

'I wasn't aware I had asked you to.'

That hurt. But then, he had intended that it should. It solved one problem, though—Amber was back to hating him again.

'Do you often take advantage of distraught women?'

His gaze was steely. 'Not often, no.'

'But it has happened?' Her voice held all the disdain she could muster.

'Possibly.' He didn't seem perturbed by Amber's obvious dislike of him; in fact he seemed to want to build on it. 'You know how it is,' he drawled laconically. 'Sexual encounters—they come and go.'

Did they? That hurt too.

She narrowed her gaze, hate building inexorably. Amber had thought his kiss had meant something. She had persuaded herself that there had been true feeling among the lust and desire. 'I can't stay here with you!'

'Are you resigning?'

Now he had her. Should she? Without even reflecting, she knew it would be the wisest, safest thing to do. But it would be the most cowardly thing too.

Amber tilted her chin defiantly. 'No.'

'Good.'

'But if you imagine for one moment that what took place just now was an indication of…of…'

He waited for Amber to find the right word, prolonging her agony, still holding her firmly against the wall, his strong, muscled body pressing against hers, tormenting her…

'You think that saying all the right things will change anything?' he demanded eventually, when it was clear that Amber couldn't find the words to continue. 'You can no more determine your destiny than I can. We want each other,' he asserted, with a deep intensity that sent shivers of desire down her spine. 'You know that and so do I.' He paused and looked deep into misted golden eyes. 'The question is…' he paused, watching her '…what do we do about it?'

CHAPTER SEVEN

AMBER told herself she should be doing something instead of just standing here, allowing Michael Hamilton to tell her things that shouldn't be true but undoubtedly were.

He was silent for a long while, just looking down into her face, considering. 'Don't look so worried.' His voice held a surprising amount of warmth, given his anger of a moment ago. 'We can work things out. Despite what you so clearly think, I'm not a lech.' A sardonic smile curved his mouth. He continued calmly, 'I'm quite able to exert control.'

He proved his point by releasing Amber's body. 'See?' He gestured slightly with his arms. 'Quite civilised.' There was a dangerous pause. 'I'm not interested in fighting with you, Amber. I have more than enough hassles in other areas of my life without making an enemy of my personal assistant.'

He looked tired, as if making his new, obviously naïve personal assistant see the light took rather too much effort.

'Is this some sort of apology?' Amber enquired coolly.

For a moment she thought he was going to be really angry. It was what she wanted—how dared he stand there talking to her as if she were some sort of foolish child? But the control he had talked about was exerted and his mouth curved into a brief smile instead. 'No, it's not. I have been known to apologise, but only when I feel I've done something wrong.'

'But—'

'Amber, let's drop the subject, shall we?' His voice was sharp, his handsome features suddenly immensely forbidding. 'I understand why you're taking this stance, and in many ways it's commendable, but if you're after an apology because I took you in my arms and kissed you then forget it!'

There was a charged silence. Amber considered her options. They were few and far between. She remembered belatedly that she was supposed to be the sort of efficient paragon that would take if not everything then a great many things in her stride.

Perhaps she ought to attempt to make this one of them.

'OK.' She tilted her chin and feigned the sort of confidence only other people felt. 'We'll call a truce.' She held out her hand and wondered if Michael would notice that it was trembling. 'Let's forget what's happened this morning,' she announced. 'I'm sure the news of Harry Vincent's heart attack threw us both off balance.'

He laughed. Damn him, he laughed! And, to make matters worse, Amber found the deep, throaty chuckle to be an immensely pleasing sound—or at least it *would* have been a pleasing sound if it hadn't indicated how easily he was amused by her.

She saw the sparkle in his eyes, understood the magnetic curve of his mouth, thought about retracting her hand—but it was too late. Strong fingers gripped her own, leaving her feeling weak and totally without a thought of her own. 'You want me as much as I want you,' he murmured smoothly. 'Why are you so frightened of admitting it?' A dark brow was raised in sardonic query. 'Is the prospect of becoming my lover so unappealing?'

Amber gaped a little. His audacity shocked her, and yet at the same time it was incredibly attractive. No one had ever spoken to her in that way before. What should she say? What would her alter ego, the efficient, take-everything-in-her-stride Miss King do? Slap him? Accuse him of sexual harassment? *What?*

She took her time replying, working hard at appearing to give the invitation some consideration. Not that she could consider it, of course; any kind of relationship would be totally out of the question. And as for sexual harassment—well, she didn't feel harassed at all. Just confused.

His gaze was full of animal vibrancy. 'No answer? Shall I take that as a don't know?'

'You can take my silence any way you choose!'

'So...' Michael regarded Amber with cool interest '...what *would* you like to do for the rest of the day?'

Amber narrowed her eyes. 'Is this a trick question? You're the boss,' she added caustically. 'I thought the idea was that you told me what to do!'

'But I've already put forward a suggestion,' Michael replied with a flash of a smile, 'and you weren't particularly impressed.'

'I can't have an affair with you!' Amber's low-voiced assertion sounded more than a little tortured. She flushed bright pink at the interrogative gaze and wished she hadn't spoken.

'Can't?' he queried. 'Or won't?'

'Look, can we please drop the subject?' she snapped irritably, struggling to free herself from his hold. 'I really just want to get back to the hotel. I...I feel exhausted.' She pushed past his large frame and hurried along the narrow side street, her high heels clattering noisily on the hard paved surface. She felt frantic, out of her depth. The unthinkable was happening and she didn't know how to stop it or what to do about it.

After a few seconds had passed, she slowed, pausing to glance in a shop window where everything sparkled. Michael was following, but at his own pace, looking devastatingly handsome, standing out head and shoulders amongst the crowds that were with them once again now that they had left the sanctuary of the Begijnhof.

Amber hovered uncertainly, waiting for his approach. Would he say anything? Sack her, maybe? In one way that would be blessed relief, and in another...

A wonderful necklace caught her eye. Amber concentrated on the scintillating circle of stones, the deepest, greenest emeralds she had ever seen, wondering what sort of woman might be lucky enough to wear such a wonderful piece of jewellery.

'Something holds special interest for you?'

'They're all very beautiful.'

'Which one in particular...?'

'Do I like?' Amber risked a glance at his face and discovered he was looking at her, not the shop window. She coloured again, and lowered her head, pointing with a finger that trembled quite noticeably. 'That one. In the middle there.'

'Good taste.' The dark head nodded in approval. 'The emeralds would look good with your hair.'

'Maybe I'll have the bracelet to match as well, then!' Amber replied lightly, desperate to introduce a note of humour and normality after the intensity of the morning.

But he wasn't listening, or if he was he chose to ignore her.

Amber followed him in silence, a pace behind, going over and over everything in a state of confused astonishment. She must not let it happen. He couldn't be kind or understanding or considerate. He *couldn't*. She told herself she hated him. She hated his aura of cool assurance. She hated his handsome face and lazy smile. She hated everything about him.

Everything.

'You look worn out. We'll hire a taxi back to the hotel.'

'I'm fine! There's absolutely no need!' She hadn't meant to snap, but snap she did.

They were alongside the canal again. Amber leant on a

rail and swept a shaky hand across her brow. She felt warm, and the water below looked so cool and inviting. It wasn't, of course—she knew that beneath the deceptively serene surface lay mud and junk and goodness knew what else—but just at that moment she longed to be submerged, to be cooled and soothed.

She glanced down at her feet, clad in smart cream shoes and silky stockings, and longed for her scruffy trainers and woolly socks.

Herself. That was what she wanted to be. Just herself.

She heard the sound of a motor launch and looked up. It was pulling alongside. Michael descended the stone steps and climbed aboard.

'Are you coming?'

'I thought you said—' And then Amber remembered. They were in Amsterdam.

It was lovely on the water, just as she had suspected it would be. The city took on another perspective. They had the craft to themselves—by design rather than accident, Amber suspected, after seeing a great many guilders pass between Michael and the driver—and it made all the difference. Amber relaxed back in her seat and looked up at the blue sky with its puffs of cloud. She could feel Michael's gaze upon her. She wondered what it was he was thinking about. But she couldn't ask. She just didn't trust herself to speak to him any more.

It was so ironic when she thought about it. How many times in her life had she tried hard to like a particularly unlikeable member of the human race? And now here she was, desperate to *hate* someone and finding it an uphill battle all the way.

'If I buy you some flowers, will you rate it as a gesture of friendship and apology rather than a tacky ploy to get you into bed?'

Amber's eyes flew open. 'What?'

'I promise I won't buy red roses.'

They were approaching the hotel. The taxi was slowing to a halt alongside a floating flower barge covered with every conceivable bloom. It was a wonderful sight, a beautiful mass of colour and perfume. Amber glanced at Michael and shook her head slightly. 'Honestly…there's no need.'

But clearly he thought there was. Michael helped her from the launch and, after a moment's discussion with the barge owner, handed her the biggest bunch of pink and white tulips she had ever laid eyes on.

Blue eyes pierced her face. 'With my regards,' he murmured huskily. 'A corny choice, maybe, but appropriate, given our location.'

'Not corny at all!' Amber touched the silky petals with her fingers. 'They're wonderful.' She looked across and met Michael's gaze. 'Thank you,' she murmured softly, 'you're very kind.'

And she found that she meant it.

She wished the lift wasn't such a problem for her. And she wished she had been more assertive and insisted on the freedom of the stairs as the hated contraption rumbled its way up towards their floor.

She stood in rigid silence, gripping her flowers before her—an ineffectual shield if ever there was one—mulling over the tiniest things, refusing to think about the big ones. Michael's kiss had been relegated to the very back of her mind. It would not do to dwell on it now. Not when he was standing so close. She concentrated hard on the numbers above the door, watching the light as it flicked from one to another.

'You OK?'

He had been watching her. Amber coloured a little and nodded. 'Fine!' She could see that the brightness of her smile didn't fool him. Not for one moment. 'I…just feel a little uncomfortable in small spaces,' she added inadequately. 'That's all.'

'You should have mentioned it,' Michael replied smoothly. 'We could have taken the stairs.'

'I'll cope. It's just a couple more floors now, isn't it?' Amber glanced back at the numbers above the door to reassure herself, following their ascent, when suddenly, without warning, the light disappeared, shortly followed by a shuddering movement as the lift jerked to an ominously silent standstill.

It had happened. Amber's worst nightmare—or one of them at least. She had been thrown off balance by the sudden, uneven movement of the lift and had stumbled towards Michael's broad frame. She jerked back in something approaching panic as her hands came into contact with his broad chest, moving away from him as if she had been stung.

She glanced above the door, her worried golden eyes mirroring her anxieties, willing the light to reappear. 'Oh, no! Please…please don't tell me it's broken down!'

Michael stepped forward and pressed a couple of buttons. He released an irritated breath. 'It looks like we're jammed between floors.'

Amber swallowed back her concern and tried to look nonchalant. 'Do you think it will be long before we get going again?' she asked quietly. 'You have pressed the emergency button?' she queried, feeling the heat of panic flushing her face. 'It's that one there, on the left by the—'

'I know which one it is,' Michael cut in mildly. 'And yes, don't worry, I've pressed it.' He considered her for a moment. 'When you mentioned a dislike for small spaces…' his tone was dry and flat, as if he was about to hear the inevitable '…I presume that was a mild way of saying you suffer from claustrophobia?'

Amber tried not to look as jumpy as she felt. 'Yes.'

A dark brow rose. 'Badly?' he queried.

She glanced round at the four walls of the lift and told herself they weren't really closing in on her. 'Bad enough,' she murmured unhappily. 'I was shut in a cupboard once, when I was quite small, by some other children. It was dark and dirty and an hour before anyone found me.'

'Relax. The hotel will get the lift fixed in no time at all.' He took a step towards her, lifted a hand and placed it gently on her flushed cheek. 'It will be all right. I promise you.' His tone was deep, calm and remarkably soothing. Amber wondered if Michael was genuinely sympathetic, or just taking that line as a precaution because he didn't fancy the idea of having to cope with a hysterical woman in a lift at the end of what had turned out to be an extremely frustrating day.

'How...do you know? We could be stuck in here for hours!'

'I doubt that.'

His calmness was suddenly infuriating. 'But you don't know!' Amber replied, unable to keep the edge from her voice. 'Don't humour me; I'm not a child!'

'OK, then, I won't. Yes, we could be stuck in here for hours! Is that what you want to hear?'

Amber lowered her gaze. 'You know it's not,' she murmured. She could still feel the scorching imprint on her face where his hand had touched her cheek. Now that it had been withdrawn she felt curiously desolate and alone.

'There's little point in getting worked up. You know as well as I that it's not going to help one bit.'

'I am *not* worked up!'

'That's good, then.' Michael's voice was suitably neutral. 'You're doing well.'

'You don't have to patronise me!' Amber sucked in a lungful of air and then wished she hadn't gulped quite so much as another awful thought struck her. 'Will we...have enough oxygen?' she asked worriedly.

'For goodness' sake!' His mouth curved into an attractive smile. 'The lift has been stationary for less than a couple of minutes.' He looked at her with benign amusement. 'Now calm down. You're beginning to look as jumpy as hell!'

'I am calm.' Amber inhaled a steadying breath and made a valiant effort to pull herself together. 'I am.'

'Good.'

There was silence. It began to have its effect. Amber glanced around the lift, trying hard to avoid the pull of Michael's gaze. She didn't succeed. It was far too strong, too intense. Neither of them spoke. Then, slowly, Michael held out his hand. She looked at the strong, capable fingers for several long seconds, her gaze lingering on the tanned skin with its manly covering of dark hair.

As a gesture of sympathy and understanding it was more effective than words could ever be. He hadn't been pretending before, Amber decided as she reached out and placed her own slender hand in his. He really did understand what she was going through.

His grasp was firm and comforting. Amber held her ground for a second or two, her arm outstretched across the few feet that distanced them. Then Michael tugged a little and she took a pace towards him.

'Let's talk,' he said. 'This is as good an opportunity as any.'

Amber moistened her lips and frowned uncertainly. 'What about?'

'You...me.' There was a pause. 'Us.'

Her heart plummeted. 'There is no...*us*.'

'Really?' He looked carefully into her anxious face. 'Are you sure about that?'

'I told you before,' she replied unhappily, 'I can't...I can't have a relationship with you.'

'Why not? Is there someone else?'

Amber shook her head slowly. 'No...but—'

'But?' Cool eyes surveyed her in sardonic amusement. 'What, then? What is it that makes you look as if you've got the weight of the world on your shoulders?'

'I just don't think it would be a good idea, that's all!' she flared defensively.

'Why don't you put the flowers down?'

Amber glanced down at the rather ragged tulips—casualties of her anxious grip. 'You bought me these as an indication of friendship and to apologise.' She looked hard at the candy-coloured blooms. 'Remember?'

'I haven't forgotten,' Michael remarked mildly. 'But who says you can't have friendship as well as a sexual relationship with someone?'

'I do.'

'Have you ever tried?'

'No!' Amber replied sharply. 'But men,' she continued self-consciously, 'or at least the ones I've come into contact with...well, they...they—'

'In your experience they've only ever been after one thing, is that it?'

Amber nodded, her lips firm. 'Exactly.'

'And you wish to include me that category?'

'I don't wish to!' She inhaled a steadying breath. 'Of course I don't!'

One dark brow was raised imperiously. 'Well, then?'

'Look, could we please just drop the subject?' Amber snapped. 'Shouldn't we be concentrating on something a little more imperative—like how we're going to get out of here?'

Amber wondered if she looked as hot as she felt. She could barely think of anything except the fact that Michael was touching her. She could feel the strength of his fingers clasped around her own; such strong, sexy hands—they seemed to her to be the embodiment of everything male.

She took another deep breath. It was becoming warm in the lift. Was it her imagination or did there definitely seem to be less air in here too?

'Are you OK? Slip off your jacket,' Michael instructed. 'I don't want you fainting on me.' He smiled. 'Although maybe it wouldn't be such a bad idea—reviving you would be an enormously pleasurable experience.'

Amber hesitated a moment, and after placing her flowers onto the floor removed her jacket. As soon as she'd done it she wished she hadn't. With bare arms and a thin blouse, there didn't seem to be enough of a barrier between Michael and her treacherous body.

It was agonising. She couldn't stop thinking about him in relation to herself. Every movement from his broad, muscular frame affected her. It was becoming difficult not to fidget. The walls seemed to be pressing in on her. It wasn't too bad when you knew you could press a button and make the doors open onto the outside world, but they were trapped in here, and as the minutes passed interminably by Amber began seriously to doubt her ability to keep calm.

'Amber, do try and keep still; pacing up and down won't get you anywhere.'

'I know that!' She released a tense breath and spun towards him angrily. 'Don't you think I know that? But it's just not that easy.' She looked nervously up at the numbers above the door in an effort to avoid looking at him, then began pacing again.

'Don't!' Michael placed a restraining hand on her arm and Amber jerked back, pressing herself against the wall of the lift, looking at him with wide, expressive eyes.

'I don't think I can take much more of this,' she whispered.

'Are you referring to the broken lift...?' he murmured softly, his gaze richly intent. 'Or something else?'

There was a heart-stopping moment of silence, then Michael took a step towards her, and as he moved inexorably closer Amber realised there was no escaping the inevitable...

Strong, sure hands cupped her face. He looked deep into her eyes and then his mouth covered hers in a slow, sensuous kiss that sent her world spinning out of control.

CHAPTER EIGHT

SUDDENLY it didn't matter that the lift wasn't working, or that Amber had promised herself she would stay strong and resolute against the onslaught of Michael Hamilton's overwhelming attraction.

His mouth drugged her with fierce kisses that screamed possession and need. His touch took all of Amber's breath away. She clung to him, gripping his jacket as he pressed his body against hers, pinning her to the wall with consummate ease.

His hands were clever and enticing, skimming her body at first, brushing over the most sensitive places, the areas where Amber's need focused itself, then repeating their journey, stronger this time, feeling the thrust as Amber pressed herself against his fingers, silently pleading with him to remove the restrictions of her clothing.

He was as aroused as she. Amber felt his hardness against her own soft body and dangerously allowed her hands to skim the tautness of thigh and buttock, pressing Michael against her in a need that was strong and at the same time faintly vulnerable.

It made him ruthless, but that didn't matter because that was what she wanted.

He kissed her mouth again, crushing her lips, thrusting his tongue against hers in imitation of the sexual act. She found herself accepting it all, but there was no time to dwell on her sanction of his lovemaking. Her need was everything. She felt as if she had been denied the intense, erotic pleasure of Michael Hamilton's body for far too long. For eternity. She wanted him so badly that it hurt.

Their mouths clashed again, and she revelled in the force of passion that powered between them. She had never before in her life been kissed like this, but it felt right—better than that, it felt wonderful.

'Michael, please!' Amber's voice didn't sound like her own. But she didn't care. She was a slave, bound to absolute obedience, and he was the master, working her hard, controlling her, showing her the way.

He kissed her again, and the thrill of desire was like a glorious pain inside. Amber slipped her hands inside his jacket, felt his broad ribcage beneath her splaying fingers, marvelled at the strength of his body, fumbled with the buttons of his shirt so that she could feel for the first time the smoothness of his skin, the roughness of the dark hair covering his chest, the firm contours of each and every muscle.

'*Michael…*' She gasped his name against the skin of his neck, clinging to him as he continued to touch her. 'Oh, Michael, I've never felt like this before.' Amber tilted her head back as his mouth scorched the skin at the base of her throat. Every nerve-end was tingling in response to his touch. All she could think of was how wonderful he made her feel. 'Please, Michael…please!' Amber pressed herself against his body, tilted her face towards his and felt his mouth on hers once again.

'Not here.' She felt his chest rise, pressing against her own as he exhaled a long, slow breath. The roughness of his cheek rested momentarily against her own.

He murmured something else, some unintelligible word that was a mix between a prayer and a curse. She felt his lips, gentler now, brushing her hair, and then Michael's hands were no longer instruments of pleasure, but of torture, leaving her body, managing somehow to exert the sort of control that Amber could only dream of.

His voice was husky when he spoke again. He cupped

Amber's face with his hands and looked deep into her eyes. 'Not like this.'

'*What?*' The whispered incredulity in her voice echoed in the confined space. Amber stiffened, mortified by his rejection; her body suddenly felt cold and empty. She tried to speak, looking up into his ruggedly handsome face with eyes that struggled to understand.

'I want you!' Michael's eyes were sharp and blue, like the sky on a cold, clear winter's morning. Icy, glacial, but burning too, marking her indelibly, so that Amber knew he was speaking the truth. 'But we can't make love here!'

'But why...?' Amber shook her head, felt humiliation rise because she had allowed so much to happen in such a short space of time. 'What was the point, then?' she demanded fiercely, struggling against sudden tears.

'There was no point.' Michael looked down as anguished eyes met his, realised that he had phrased it badly and added urgently, 'I mean that it wasn't premeditated. You know that, surely? Don't make it sound as if it were some kind of test.' He shook his head and there was bewilderment in his gaze, as if he too could hardly believe how far things had progressed between them. 'You were just so... so...'

'So what?' Amber glared at him. 'Pathetic? Naïve? And you decided to take advantage!' Her voice was as hard as stone.

'That's not the way it was!' Michael's expression mirrored her tone. 'And you know it!' He paused a moment. 'For God's sake, listen!' he instructed harshly.

Amber was quiet, and in the silence a faint rumbling could be heard, the sound of cables and pulleys moving overhead. 'The lift's being mended,' Michael informed her tersely. '*Now* do you understand?' His voice was low; the remains of passion still lingered around the edges of each word that he spoke. 'Those doors could have opened at any time and then how would you have felt?'

'I know how I feel now,' Amber whispered.

Disappointed, cheated…dreadfully, dreadfully frustrated.

'You think I'm not feeling the same way?' Michael glanced down at her body and Amber's face burned as his eyes lingered on her skin. 'You'd better cover yourself,' he added, 'and quickly.'

It was an order that needed to be obeyed. Amber's hands trembled as she smoothed down her skirt. Michael helped without being asked, buttoning the front of her blouse, brushing back the many errant strands of hair from her face. Then he bent his head and kissed her, his mouth moving slowly over her mouth, drugging her all over again, making her want him, torturing her because she knew it couldn't happen—not here anyway.

'You'd better put this on,' he drawled huskily, picking up her jacket from the floor. 'You still look a little dishevelled.'

She lowered her gaze and blushed furiously, then took the jacket with shaking hands and slipped it on quickly, making sure it was pulled close.

'Look at me!' Michael's voice held a sharp edge of command. One finger tipped her chin so that the large golden eyes would look into the demanding face. 'This isn't the end,' he informed her steadily. 'We *will* finish what we've started.'

He meant what he said, and Amber was glad—she couldn't lie to herself a moment longer. She wanted him. She couldn't stop thinking about him. If he had jammed the lift doors and proceeded to remove her clothes one by one, touched her body, kissed her mouth, she would have been powerless to stop him, to stop herself.

But he hadn't and there was no more time to think or react because the lift shuddered into life at that moment and in the next few seconds the doors were sliding open and there in front of them stood a small crowd of apologetic workmen and the hotel manager.

They got off lightly. Given another time, another situation, Amber knew that Michael would have lambasted the lot of them for incompetence. As it was, he accepted the manager's profuse apologies with cool detachment, and then informed him that he did not expect to be presented with a bill and that he would be leaving the hotel within the hour.

'Why?'

'Why what?' Michael frowned as he looked down into her face. They were outside the door to Amber's room.

'You told the manager we'd be leaving immediately,' she replied quietly. 'Did you mean it?'

'Of course.'

'Oh…' She tried not to look hurt, but it wasn't that easy. What had she expected? For Michael to take her in his arms as soon as they were alone again?

She hovered uncertainly. 'Michael—'

'I'll go to my room. Can you be ready in an hour?'

She couldn't believe he was doing this to her—not after what had just occurred between them. He sounded so…so normal. Whilst she was still reliving every moment of passion in the lift, Michael was looking ahead, thinking about his plans in London.

'Ten minutes if that's what you require—*sir*!' she added harshly.

'Don't look at me like that.' Michael released a breath and threw her a warning glance. 'I'm not trying to hurt you,' he added roughly.

'Aren't you?' Amber's eyes flashed fire. 'Well, you may not be trying, but you're sure as hell managing to do a good job of it!'

He took a step towards her, but Amber backed away,

presenting him with a face that was hard and cold and full
of defiance.

He grimaced. 'Do you think this is any easier for me?
Do you think I *expected* this to happen?'

'Frankly, yes! Yes, I do,' Amber replied tightly. 'Wasn't
Amsterdam meant to be the city where you mixed business
and pleasure?'

'That was an off-the-cuff remark and you know it!' He
looked angry, but Amber forced herself to continue, to really ruin everything.

'Do I?' she cried. 'You kissed me on the dance floor, in
front of Harry Vincent and his girlfriend, and it was absolutely premeditated; you know it was!'

'That was different. Totally and utterly different.'
Michael's jaw clenched. Slowly he shook his head. 'You
really don't trust me an inch, do you? *Do you?*' he demanded.

Amber hesitated badly. She didn't know what to say. Her
head, where the last vestige of common sense remained,
reminded her of Beatrice, of the main reason, the *only* reason, she had ever got herself mixed up in all of this. Whilst
her heart... Well, what had happened to that? *What?*

'Nothing to say?' Michael observed her for a moment in
silence. 'That's why I think it would be best if we leave
this hotel, this city.' He paused, holding her gaze ruthlessly.
'If I made love to you now, it wouldn't be the same, would
it?' he asked.

'Who said I'd let you?' Amber held her jacket tightly
around her body, saw the steel in Michael's gaze and acknowledged the truth of his words. 'No,' she added quietly.
'No, it wouldn't.'

'So pack...have a bath. Let's get out of here.'

'Don't tell me what to do! Don't stand there and talk to
me as if I'm little more than an employee after what's just
happened between us!'

Did anyone else dare to speak to him like that? She didn't know or care. All she knew was that she *had* to if she wanted to keep a modicum of self-respect. 'I'm quite capable of organising my own life!' Amber gritted angrily. 'I don't need you or your dubious charms!' Her voice was taut with strain. They weren't employer and employee any longer. They were lovers—almost anyway.

A dangerous silence filled the space between them. When Michael spoke, his voice was as hard as granite, matching the steely glint in his eyes. 'My charms—dubious or otherwise—seemed to appeal a moment ago,' he delivered coolly. 'Funny,' he continued, not looking the least bit amused, 'but I was under the impression that we understood one another.'

'You'll never understand me!' Amber's voice shook with the intensity of her words. 'Never!'

'I'm beginning to believe that that might be true.'

She turned from him, so that he wouldn't see the tears in her eyes, but he caught hold of her and spun her back around to face him.

'You know, fighting with me won't change anything,' he asserted. 'You'll still want me.'

'You are so arrogant!' Amber shook her head, her eyes blazing. 'How can you say such a thing?'

'Because it's true.' His mouth hardened. 'Or are you going to play games and pretend that it isn't?'

'I don't even like you,' she croaked, with something approaching weariness.

'But you want me.' He paused. 'And I want you. But not here. Not like this.'

Amber didn't know whether to feel relief or despair. Michael Hamilton still wanted her. He looked sensational—strong and handsome. Determined. He leant forward then, catching Amber off guard. 'We *will* work it out,' he murmured huskily, kissing her partly opened mouth with slow assurance. 'I promise you that.'

'Are you feeling OK?'

'Fine.'

She wasn't. Amber was on edge like never before, but somehow she managed to feign a relaxed position, shifting her body in the reclining seat as the plane levelled off and headed towards England.

Michael sat opposite her. Papers were strewn on the low table between them. Was he really as engrossed in business as he pretended? she wondered. It seemed so. Amber eyed him surreptitiously from beneath a fringe of dark lashes and watched as he read, pausing to make notes from time to time, shifting pieces of paper from one pile to another as he dealt with each of them.

It was so easy for him. Surely that should have been warning enough?

She *had* to resist. That much was clear. For her own sake as well as for Beatrice's. There must be no continuation of the madness that had assailed her in Amsterdam. For how would she be able to face her own sister, a sister who was depending on her to do what was right, if she allowed herself to be seduced by the very man who had destroyed that sister's happiness?

Amber closed her eyes. The images were strong and vivid and they shocked her, but she forced herself to think about them. He would make love to her once, maybe twice if she was lucky. She wasn't naïve enough to assume that Michael Hamilton would want to continue their liaison for any real length of time. His desire, his *lust*, would be satisfied after the briefest of sexual encounters; he would love her and leave her—more than likely sack her—and Amber would be left feeling humiliated...hating herself.

No, they weren't business colleagues, they weren't

friends and they would never, *could* never be lovers—not in the true sense of the word.

'Asleep, or just deep in thought?'

Her eyes shot open at the sound of Michael's voice. 'Neither,' she replied neutrally. 'I was just resting.'

He regarded her steadily for a moment. 'You look pretty worn out,' he asserted. 'I was going to run through a couple of things with you...' He lifted a sheaf of papers from the table in indication of what he meant. 'But perhaps it would be better left until Monday.'

'No, now's fine!' Amber inhaled swiftly and modified the tone of her voice to something a little less urgent, less desperate. 'Honestly,' she added, 'I'd rather concentrate on work.'

'Than what?' He wasn't going to let her forget. With him sitting opposite looking so ruggedly handsome, she *couldn't* forget.

'I wonder how Harry Vincent is doing?' Amber replied swiftly, determined to change the subject. 'I wish we'd found out before we left Amsterdam.'

'I did.' Michael slapped another buff-coloured folder down onto a pile.

'Really?' Amber didn't try to hide her surprise. 'When?'

'I phoned whilst you were packing.'

Another incident to indicate how little their encounter in the lift had meant, Amber thought. Whilst she had been struggling to think straight, Michael had been ringing the hospital. 'And?' She thrust the depressing thought away, her eyes carefully wandering over his face. 'Is he all right?'

'He came through the emergency operation as well as could be expected. They said he was out of danger.'

'Oh, thank goodness!' Amber couldn't help feeling a little guilty. She had barely given Harry Vincent a thought since that morning.

'I sent some flowers and fruit; I'm not sure he's in any position to appreciate them, though.'

'I'm your personal assistant; I should have done it.' Her voice was quiet. She stared down at her lap, then looked up and met Michael's impassive gaze. 'Why didn't you ask me?'

'Because it didn't seem appropriate—not at the time,' he replied crisply. 'You weren't exactly thinking coherently, were you?'

'I...I can't believe...I mean...what happened in the lift...' Amber stumbled over her words, feeling foolish. 'It shouldn't have happened,' she finished firmly.

'Care to tell me why not?' It was a casual enquiry. Michael's expression spoke volumes; 'idle scrutiny' just about summed it up. He could have been discussing a minor difference of opinion instead of the most passionate encounter that Amber had ever experienced in her life.

But of course. There was the difference; for her it had been a moment of world-shattering importance, for him probably no more than an extremely pleasant diversion.

'*Amber!* Will you please talk to me?'

'I don't think I've got anything more to say,' she murmured stiffly. 'Will you sack me when we get back to England?' *Please!* she cried silently.

'You're worried about your position?' Michael's voice was crisp. 'You have no need. I don't renege on my promises. I said a month's trial and that's what you'll receive.'

'How kind of you to reassure me!' She couldn't keep the sting from her voice. Did he really think she cared about that? 'So you'll treat me fairly whether I sleep with you or not?' she asked, mustering a remarkably calm, conversational tone to rival his own. 'How gallant you are!'

There was a huge silence. 'You really don't like me, do you?' He looked only mildly intrigued. Not hurt or embarrassed, just surprised.

'No. As a matter of fact...' Amber struggled uncomfortably to find a suitable word, aware of Michael's watchful gaze. 'No,' she whispered. 'No, I don't think I do.'

'And why is that? Do you mind if I ask?' he added, with cool sarcasm.

Amber released a taut breath, hating the way the conversation was going. 'It's a matter of...of character,' she replied finally.

'Yours or mine?'

She was getting deeper and deeper into a mess. What had someone once said? When you find yourself in a hole, stop digging... Amber decided that that was a very sound piece of advice and promptly clamped her mouth shut.

'Diplomacy at this late stage?' Glacial blue eyes mocked her. 'Hardly worth the effort, surely?'

'I'm a professional,' she replied at last. 'Or at least I thought I was. You're not making this very easy.'

'*I'm* not?' He slanted her a look of impatience. 'Would you care to tell me what the real problem is here? *Well?*' he demanded roughly, when Amber made no reply. 'Tell me! Why are you acting like this? Oh, come on!' His voice was hard and cold, like steel. He threw the file he was holding angrily down onto the table, and papers fell out and scattered everywhere.

A reaction at last, Amber thought. Was that progress or not?

'Speak to me!' He glared at her. 'You think I'm a complete and utter bastard! That I take what I want, when I want it, without regard for anyone's feelings except my own! Isn't that the truth of the matter?'

She wanted to cry. His anger was harsh and sudden. Tears stung her eyes, threatened to spill onto her cheeks. Twice—three times in one day. And all because of this man. She usually never cried. Never.

It was no use. She couldn't defend herself. Amber rose from her seat.

'Where are you going?' His voice was rough.

'I...I don't know. Anywhere!' she croaked. 'Away from you.'

'You're headed towards the cockpit; I don't think the pilot will appreciate the distraction,' Michael snapped. 'There's the galley, but that will be rather cramped—barely room enough for you and the steward.'

'Maybe I'd be better throwing myself out of the window, then!' Amber replied tightly.

'For a cool, controlled professional, you certainly tend to go for the dramatic angle, don't you?' Michael replied tightly. He rose from his seat and advanced inexorably towards her as he spoke, unsmiling as Amber glanced around frantically. 'If you're looking for a way out, there's just one more place left to hide.'

He was close. She glanced up into the determined, handsome face, not knowing how to feel. 'Where?' she croaked.

'I have a cabin where I rest on long hauls,' he murmured. 'It's small but extremely comfortable.'

'No!' Amber shook her head, but her protests were lost as Michael pulled her into his arms and then, astonishingly, lifted her clean off her feet. 'Put me down!' she cried wildly. 'What do you think you're doing?'

'What does it look like?' he drawled, seemingly unaffected by her anger. 'I'm taking you to my cabin.'

'But you...you can't!'

'I can and I will.'

'You think you can act like this because of what happened between us in the lift?' Amber demanded. 'Well, you can't! I won't allow it.'

'You're overdramatising again,' he informed her flatly. 'You honestly believe I'd seduce you now, like this?' He looked down into her face and shook his head. 'You'd have every right to think me a bastard then, wouldn't you? You're overwrought,' he informed her firmly as he pushed open a discreet door at the far end of the main room and dropped her onto a compact mattress in an extremely well-designed sleeping space. 'Get some rest.'

Amber looked up at him from her crouched, foetal position on the bed. His frame was broad and strong and hugely impressive in the confines of the small cabin. 'Do you expect me to say thank you,' she asked defiantly, 'because you decided against seduction?'

It was a dangerous thing to say—Amber could hardly believe it was she who had uttered such provocative words. She glanced fearfully up into Michael's face, saw the look of danger lingering in his eyes.

'I could always change my mind,' he drawled. 'Is that what you'd prefer, Amber?' He crouched down beside the bed, reached out a hand and cupped her chin firmly between his fingers. 'Let's see, shall we?'

His mouth covered her lips with smooth assurance, enticing them apart, moving with deliberate intent, removing all ideas of resistance from her thoughts. She could have struggled and protested, but she didn't. The moment his mouth covered hers she was lost. Total defeat. She wanted him.

But he didn't want her—not at that moment anyway. Maybe never again. Michael withdrew his mouth from hers as soon as her lips had parted in supplication, as soon as Amber had closed her eyes and covered the hand that held her face with her own.

'Too easy.' He shook his head, punishing her. 'Get some sleep,' he ordered. 'I'll have the steward wake you when we reach London.'

CHAPTER NINE

SHE didn't sleep. It was doubtful whether Michael had even expected her to. Amber sat up and wondered what she should do. Going over and over everything a thousand times didn't bring the answers that she had hoped for.

There was a small built-in dressing table opposite the bed and she looked closely at her own reflection, critical of her fine, porcelain-like complexion and soft, slightly pouting mouth. Nothing on the surface to indicate madness, she thought; just an average-looking girl with thick auburn hair and golden eyes. But she knew she was insane even if it didn't show—she must be to still want Michael Hamilton so much, despite everything.

There was a brief knock on the door and it opened. Amber's heart leapt and then fell, deflated, as a white-coated steward informed her they would be landing shortly.

She emerged a moment later, having aborted her attempt to do something about her tousled appearance.

Michael was in his seat, drink at hand, reading a report from a file balanced on his lap. He had probably hardly noticed she had been away. He didn't look up when Amber sat down opposite him. So she fastened her seat belt with a snap and pretended it didn't matter.

The landing was a little bumpy. Amber gripped the arm of her seat and wished that the whole doomed trip was at an end, and she was tucked safely up in her own bed in her own cramped little flat.

He didn't speak to her. Not as they exited the plane or as the chauffeured limousine drove efficiently and silently through the wet, depressing streets to the outskirts of

London. It was only when the car was brought to a stand-still and the driver got out and opened her door that he deigned to say anything.

'Will I see you on Monday?'

She looked across the expanse of leather upholstery. She had been asking herself that very question ever since the plane had landed, and she still didn't know the answer.

She glanced hopelessly around the swish interior of the car, avoiding the dominating figure, her eyes just skimming the long, powerful legs that were stretched out in stark contrast against the cream-coloured seat.

The chauffeur was waiting patiently. He would stand there holding the door for as long as it took, because Michael Hamilton paid him to and that was his job. The grey hair and lined face indicated he was old enough to be her father. If he knew the facts he would probably tell her to get out while she still could, whilst she had her sanity still intact. For that was what was at stake—her mind. Her body had already fallen; Michael Hamilton could take control of that whenever he pleased. Her mind was the only thing that she had left to protect.

Amber felt depression swoop down and catch her in its claws. What was the use? What was the point in pretending that she could make a difference?

Revenge. What a stupid, stupid idea.

'I'd appreciate an answer.' His voice was smooth. 'I need to know where I stand.'

Did he care what she did? Amber wondered. Would it matter to him if she never showed her face again? She averted her gaze, closing her eyes briefly in something approaching silent prayer, then she turned back towards Michael and nodded briefly. 'Yes,' she replied quietly. 'I'll be there.'

Her summons came an hour after she'd arrived at the office on Monday morning. Amber knocked cautiously on the polished wooden door and waited for the sound of Michael's voice. She felt sick with nerves and about as inefficient and unprofessional as it was possible to be. She was extremely smart, though, dressed in yet another of Carol's suits—this one in navy with a long bias-cut skirt which swirled demurely around the middle of her calves. Her white blouse was crisp, and looked good against the fitted jacket and matching suede shoes.

Once again a transformation had been effected. On the inside she was still the out-of-work teacher who liked to lounge around in jeans and sweatshirt and enjoyed a secret vice of eating ice cream straight from the carton, but on the outside she was a professional woman who had to assert herself and look as if she could handle the situation that was about to be presented to her.

She was going to have to resign. She couldn't go on with this dreadful charade. Sooner or later she was going to have to make the decision never to see Michael Hamilton again.

He looked as stunning as ever. It was already apparent to Amber, from the conversations she had enjoyed around the offices so far, that virtually every female, with the possible exception of the dour and aged Miss Jones, lusted after him with a vengeance. Impeccably dressed in an excellent dark suit, sleek black hair swept back from his tanned, autocratic face, he was the epitome of wealth and power and unconscious style.

Is that why I'm attracted to him? Amber asked herself swiftly as she crossed the huge expanse of neutral-coloured carpet on legs that felt like jelly. Am I the same as all the other girls? Is it really just about image and power and looks?

'Morning.' He looked at her and she returned his gaze impassively, looking at him, unable to stop herself thinking about what her life would be like when this man, whom she barely knew, was no longer a part of it...

'We'll pretend for the moment, shall we?' he delivered flatly. 'We'll pretend that you are just my personal assistant and I am just your employer. Is that what you want?'

Amber nodded as relief flooded through her. 'Yes,' she murmured. 'Yes, please.'

'Any important messages?' His voice was suddenly brisk and businesslike. He lowered his dark head as he spoke, to continue work on yet another report.

'Er...' Amber scanned her memory and wondered how he expected her to differentiate between important and not so important calls at this early stage. 'No,' she finished firmly. 'I've pencilled in some appointments, though, for later in the week.'

He looked up briefly then, meeting her nervous gaze, hard blue eyes telling her that business was the only thing on his mind. 'What's happening today?'

Amber slipped the large black leather diary, a duplicate of the one on Michael's desk, from under her arm and listed the various meetings that had been scheduled. It was a long list, taking him right up until early evening with what seemed like barely a pause for thought.

'Anything else?'

Wasn't that enough? Amber wondered. 'No, I don't think so.'

'I need some files.' He reeled off a list at bullet speed, watching without comment whilst Amber frantically scribbled the names down as fast as she could manage. 'I also want you to put through some calls for me.' He held out a piece of paper. 'I'd like to talk to these people. Any order— it doesn't matter. Oh, and you'll need to call someone in to fix my coffee-machine—it's broken.'

She glanced across the room and noted the table where the defunct machine stood idle. 'What's wrong with it?'

'It's not heating.' He didn't bother to raise his head from his work. He was engrossed. Amber waited a moment, and when it was apparent that there were no more orders she made the lengthy journey back across the carpet and left the room.

She sat down at her untidy desk in the outer office and stared into space dejectedly. The proverb about having one's cake and eating it forced its way into Amber's mind. OK, so she was being perverse—hadn't she prayed time and again over the last twenty-four hours that Michael would put no pressure on her? But having him speak to her without feeling now, ignoring the fact that they...well, that they had been as close to being lovers as it was possible to get without actually... Well, it just wasn't as easy as she had imagined.

The intercom on Amber's desk buzzed impatiently.

'Have you got those calls ready for me yet?'

She glanced at the screwed-up piece of paper in her hand and smoothed it out hurriedly. 'I'm just about to see to it now,' she replied crisply, emulating his tone.

By late afternoon she was a seething, nervous wreck. It had been the sort of day that would have tested a saint, and as Amber was nowhere near being a devout, heavenly individual she was in an extremely bad mood.

Nothing had gone smoothly; 'unhelpful' was definitely Miss Jones's middle name, and Michael had barely given her time to draw breath before burdening her with yet more tasks.

By six-thirty most of the staff had gone home. Amber was still struggling to complete work on yet another report, frantically gathering together pieces of information that had seemingly been scattered to the four winds, and she doubted very much whether she'd make it to the haven of her flat much before nightfall.

An hour later the pages were finally in a logical order.

Amber was just allowing herself a small degree of satisfaction when the intercom on her desk buzzed loudly in the now quiet office. Startled by the sound, she reached forward hastily to press the button and succeeded in somehow knocking an unfinished cup of cold coffee all over the carefully arranged pile of papers. As if in slow motion, she watched the soggy sheets slide one by one, like a waterfall, over the edge of her messy desk onto the floor.

She shrieked aloud, hardly caring that Michael would probably be deafened by the sound, as she stared down at the carpet in dismay, thinking of all the hours of hard work that she had put in.

'What on earth is going on?' His voice buzzed irritably through the intercom, but she didn't have the energy to reply. Amber continued to stare trance-like at the floor. Even when the connecting door was opened sharply and Michael appeared she made no move. Tears slid silently down her cheeks—huge, moist drops that were cool against her flushed, frantic cheeks and tasted of salt.

'*Amber?*' From the tone of his voice, it sounded as if Michael could hardly believe his eyes.

Her gaze shifted from the floor to the top of her desk. The mess said it all. Never before, probably never again, would the Hamilton Corporation employ such an incompetent PA.

'This is the report I've been waiting for?' he enquired tersely, crouching down to lift a couple of soggy brown pages in continued disbelief. 'You do know how important this information is, I suppose?'

She moved her head slightly, as if in a daze. 'I think so,' she murmured wearily. 'I've been working on it all afternoon.'

'So you have!' Michael replied crisply. 'And I've been waiting for it all afternoon too!' He let out a sigh which spoke volumes. Amber waited, wondering if he'd shout, or humiliate her with a few well-chosen words. 'Oh, for good-ness' sake, stop crying; it's not the end of the world!' It was an order, not a gesture of sympathy.

Amber hung her head and scrubbed away her tears with the back of her hand. 'It is to me,' she sobbed. 'I'm useless. Utterly useless!'

'Look at me.'

That was the one thing she didn't want to do. He would see it all in her face: the unprofessional inefficiency, the humiliation of not being up to the job, the fact that she had missed his company all through the long day.

She might have known he would use force. Strong, com-manding fingers tilted her chin until she had no choice but to look him straight in the face. 'Bad day, huh?'

'What do you think?' Amber struggled with the sob that was caught at the back of her throat and then nodded. 'Dreadful,' she murmured miserably.

'I've put you through it, haven't I?' He looked at her with an expression of sympathy. 'Let me take you home.'

'But…what about the report?' She sounded like a child. Amber had a sudden, overwhelming desire to throw herself at Michael and sob uncontrollably. She needed his strength; she wanted, with a desperation that astounded and ashamed her, to feel his arms around her weary, inadequate body.

'It can wait until the morning.'

'But you said—'

'I know what I said.' His eyes were cool and penetrating. 'But we can't always have what we want, can we? I think I've worked that much out by now.'

Amber met his gaze. 'You're not giving me the sack?'

'Do you think I should?'

She was exhausted, but Amber still wanted him. Being this close, hearing the deep, even tones of his voice, seeing the way his eyes consumed her face left her feeling dizzy with need. She didn't like feeling inadequate.

LAURA MARTIN   129

'I...I want to carry on with the report,' she announced
defiantly. She moved her head backwards and found it easier to think now that Michael wasn't actually touching her.
'I was clumsy,' she added. 'It's my fault it's in a mess. '
She pushed her chair out of the way and crouched down
to retrieve the papers. 'I can reprint them from the computer; it shouldn't take too long.'

A large, tanned hand covered hers suddenly, preventing
her from gathering them up. Amber looked sideways. 'You
don't have to do this!' he told her quietly.

But of course they both knew by then that she did.

'There! Finished!' Amber placed the thick volume down
on Michael's desk with a flourish. She had worked like a
demon, and a surprisingly efficient one at that. And this
time, despite her tiredness and frustration, everything had
gone far more smoothly.

'You work better when there are no distractions, I see,'
Michael delivered conversationally. He picked up the pages
without giving them so much as a glance and placed them
into the open briefcase on his desk.

'But aren't you going to look at it?' Amber queried, disappointed by his lack of interest.

'I will. Later.'

She watched as Michael lifted his jacket from the back
of his chair and switched off the brass lamp on his desk.
The whole complexion of the office felt different now that
there was less light. It had an atmospheric quality, softer,
dusky. Through the large windows, the lights of the city
could be seen twinkling like stars.

'You're going home?' Amber's voice was subdued.

'That's right.' Michael clicked the case shut and picked
it up, rounding the desk towards her. 'Are you coming?'

All at once she forgot about her disastrous day and the
mess she had made of everything. He was close to her, and

the darkness seemed to add to his presence rather than detract from it, outlining the broadness of his frame, accentuating the strong line of his jaw, darkening his hair and his suit so that the whiteness of his shirt and the smooth, tanned skin of his face stood out in contrast.

'Amber?' His eyes scanned her face in the dim light, questioning her. He didn't move, but then he didn't have to; his eyes and voice did all the work, reeling her in, holding her, trapping her in an invisible net of sexual awareness. 'I said I'd take you home.'

'It's all right.' Amber backed towards the door, suddenly conscious of the dangers that surrounded her. 'I can catch the tube.'

'I'm sure you can, but I won't allow it. I've already said I'll give you a lift.'

'And I've told you that I'm quite capable of finding my own way home!' Why was she being so difficult? Against the luxury of riding in a chauffeur-driven limousine, the delights of public transport didn't really stand a chance. It was because he had ignored her all day. She felt hurt. She knew full well that she was being ridiculously contrary, but her pride was damaged. It had been *easy* for him. More than twelve long hours with only a door between them and Michael had continued his working day as if her presence made no difference.

She wrenched open the door, conscious of his broad frame close behind her. In the brighter lights of the outer office everyday life continued; Amber glanced along the corridor and caught sight of the army of cleaners working their way towards them.

'Do you want to make a fuss about it out here?' he enquired with deceptive mildness. 'I'm not going to take no for an answer. I'm even prepared to resort to underhand means just so that you'll say yes.'

'You wouldn't!'

The attractive mouth curved; he moved a fraction closer, showing her. 'Do you want to try me?' he drawled. 'It would liven up the cleaners' evening, I'm sure!'

'I'll go with you, then,' Amber replied swiftly, stepping back so that there was space between them, her expression deliberately hard so that he wouldn't get the wrong idea, imagine for one moment that she was pleased to accept his offer. 'If you insist.'

They were in his own Mercedes and Michael was driving— the chauffeured limousine having been sent home long ago. The interior smelt of leather and wood, with a hint of cologne and the general opulence that was part and parcel of his expensive lifestyle.

Amber had been intent on her own thoughts for the past few minutes; now she glanced out of the car window at the swish neighbourhood—tall, beautifully proportioned houses, each with a glossy black door and neat black railings—and felt a sudden rush of panic. 'This isn't the way to my flat. You said you'd take me home.'

'And so I shall—but later.'

She worked immensely hard at keeping her voice level, and failed. 'All I want,' she replied unsteadily, 'is a hot bath, a change of clothes and some food.'

'Who says you won't be able to get those things at my place?'

She stared at him in wide-eyed amazement, hardly able to believe his presumption. 'You think...' she began. 'You think that...that—'

'That you are extremely tired and you need to be pampered a little.' He glanced across at her. 'What's the problem? You're looking at me as if I'm some kind of madman.' Michael manoeuvred the vehicle around a car waiting to park at the side of the road. He smiled briefly. 'Did you really imagine I'd just drive you home and drop you?'

'Yes,' she replied stiffly. 'As a matter of fact I did.'

'You really don't understand me, do you? You think I've chosen to forget about Amsterdam?'

'Maybe *I'm* the one who's decided to forget it!' Amber replied sharply. 'Have you considered that?'

'The thought did cross my mind, but only briefly,' Michael delivered casually. 'One look at you this morning told me you had been thinking about it just as much as I had.'

'Michael...' Amber shook her head. 'You can't do this to me! I won't...allow it.'

'And what exactly is it I'm going to do?' His eyes were upon her. His voice was deep and husky, challenging her, defying her to voice her concerns aloud.

He had stopped the car. They looked at one another for a long while, without speaking. His question reverberated around inside her head. What was he going to do?

He opened the car door and got out. 'Are you coming in?'

She shook her head, stubborn to the last. She wanted Beatrice to be proud of her. 'No.'

'There's no need to look at me like that,' Michael drawled. 'I won't jump on you as soon as you're past the front door. If called upon, I can exert perfect control—you know that.'

Amber pursed her lips angrily. She stayed where she was, even as Michael walked away. Frowning, she watched through the windscreen as he ascended stone steps and thrust a key into a glossy front door. She waited, expecting him to glance around, but he didn't.

The swish Knightsbridge home was opened. She caught a glimpse of a pale wall and a vibrant piece of modern art and then he entered, leaving Amber sitting alone in the car in the dusky street, staring at the lure of the open door.

She sat in the car for five minutes, debating. Pride was

involved, of course, but that faded into insignificance when compared with the other issues.

She wanted him. But Michael Hamilton's possession would come at a price. Her virginity for one, her sanity for another. There had been men in her life before now, but none important enough to commit herself to. Boys really— that was all they had been. Just boys. Easygoing, naïve, fun. She thought about Michael.

He was none of those things. Was that what attracted her—the danger?

Amber released a long-drawn-out sigh. If she felt confused now, it would be nothing to how she would feel afterwards. Would she feel elated? Fulfilled? Instinct told her it would be both of those. But what about later, when the afterglow of their lovemaking had worn off? Cheated? Hurt? Used?

'I don't know him,' Amber whispered. But I want to, she thought, looking across at his house. I do. Very much.

Her fingers shook as she fumbled for the door catch. Her legs trembled as she cautiously crossed the pavement and ascended the stone steps. Once she crossed the threshold it would be difficult to turn back. Curiously enough, it wasn't Michael she was frightened of, it was herself. She believed his claim about exerting control—if she said no, he would abide by her decision.

The scene in the lift sprang into life in her memory. Amber's stomach stirred with the power of it. Saying no— that would be the difficult thing.

She slipped through the front door, peering around its edge cautiously, glancing along the impressive hallway, aware in some far off corner of her mind of strategically placed pieces of art—flashes of brilliant colour in a monochrome setting.

It was very quiet. Amber's shoes made too much noise on the black and white tiles.

Michael was in the living room, pouring a drink. Two glasses, Amber noticed. He had known she would come. He turned as she entered and she found herself catching her breath. The power of his effect on her was a continual surprise. He was a dark, impressive figure, sharp against the pale walls and furniture.

'For you.' His voice was smooth and deep. He held out a glass, walking towards her, not allowing her to escape from the depth of his gaze for one moment. 'You look as if you could do with a drink.'

'Do you always get what you want?' Amber enquired stiltedly.

'Not always, no.' His eyes were burning into her face. Such power, she thought dejectedly. How am I supposed to fight this?

She accepted the wineglass he offered, gripping it tightly in both hands. 'You have a nice house,' she murmured, taking a sip, glancing round at the huge, sparsely furnished room, listening with a sinking heart to her own, inane words. 'It's distinctive. Uncluttered.'

'An element I try to incorporate wherever possible.' His voice was dark and serious. 'Keep things simple; life's much easier that way.'

What about Beatrice? Did he consider that his attempted seduction of her had been an easy option? And of herself?

She waited, expecting the thought to have an effect, to make her change her mind about being here in Michael Hamilton's home, but it didn't.

'You look thoughtful suddenly.' He slanted her a look. 'Anything serious? I find myself wondering often about what's going on in that mind of yours,' he added, when Amber made no reply. 'I know there's definitely more to you than meets the eye.'

'How do you know?'

'I told you when we first met that I'm an expert reader

of body language.' His tone was light, but it didn't fool Amber for one moment. 'Why don't you tell me what's bothering you?'

He hadn't kissed her. He hadn't even touched her. Was it a conscious decision, Amber wondered, or hadn't the thought or the desire crossed his mind?

She felt confused. Unsure. Totally and utterly out of her depth. All at once she wanted Michael to take her in his arms. The need was like a pain in the pit of her stomach.

What would Bea think of her now—silently lusting after the man who had ruined her life?

'I...I can't!'

He frowned at the anguish in her voice, hesitated then said, 'Why don't you go upstairs? Make yourself at home, have a bath.'

Amber's eyes narrowed. Just like that? He really expected her to do it? To go upstairs, strip off, wallow upstairs in a tub full of scented bubbles? Was that what all his women did?

'Why me?' she asked.

He didn't insult her by pretending not to understand. 'Because you're beautiful...sweet...vulnerable.'

'I'm sure you've used those words before.' She raised her eyebrows. She was trembling like a leaf inside, but she was determined to present a cool front. 'That's it?'

'No.' His eyes darkened, matching the tone of his voice. 'But I can't explain the rest.'

'Can't or won't?'

He smiled—a sensuous curve of his mouth which made her leaden heart leap in response. 'Both.'

She hardened her heart. What was the use in fooling herself? 'I'm a novelty; I'm stubborn and I dare to argue,' she replied flatly. 'You find it intriguing.'

'And you're an expert on the ways of men, are you?'

Michael demanded sharply. 'You know everything there is to know?'

'Tell me it isn't true, then,' Amber said quietly. 'Go on, do it! Lie! I'm not a fool. There's no way you'll convince me.'

'I want us to be lovers. You want the same thing.'

Her mouth twisted into a painful smile. 'Too simple,' she murmured. 'Far too simple.'

'Does it have to be so damned complicated, then?' He shook his head and looked at her with a hard expression. 'I've had women—lots of them,' he continued stonily. 'Too many, perhaps. And when I look back I realise that most of them have merged into one—an indistinct mass of blonde or dark heads with smiling red mouths who always...*always*,' he repeated with hard emphasis, 'said yes.'

'Is there a point to this revelation?' Amber's voice sounded strangulated. 'Am I supposed to *enjoy* hearing this?'

Michael's mouth firmed into a hard line. 'I'm trying to explain—'

'There's no need!' Her tone was harsh; vivid pictures of Michael and any number of glamorous women were torturing her beyond belief.

'I think there is!'

'I'm sorry.' Amber placed her glass down on a black onyx surface with a bang. 'I can't listen to this. I have to go. I don't expect you to take me home. This is my fault. I made the mistake in coming here. I'll call a taxi.' She turned and half ran across the room, knocking into an elegant side table as she went, hearing the clatter as it hit the floor behind her.

Her high-heeled shoes skidded in the hallway. Her heart was pounding. She heard Michael call her name and moved even faster towards the front door.

'Amber!' He caught up with her just as she had opened

the door. It was banged shut, the catch flying out of her grasp as Michael caught hold of her body and swung her around to face him. 'What's the matter?'

'You have to ask that?' Amber scanned his face, confusion turning to dislike, dislike to hate, as she thought of what he had put her through. 'I'm not that sort of girl!' she gritted. 'I can't…'

She shook her head, angry that the right words wouldn't come. 'It doesn't mean a thing to you, does it?' she demanded. 'Not a thing! Just sex! Just pleasure. Well, that's OK! But not with me. Not with me!' She struggled to free herself from his hold, but his hands were too strong. 'I can't alter my feelings to suit the occasion!'

'And what *do* you feel?' His eyes were burning into her face. Cold, sharp flints of ice that wouldn't release her until she gave him a truthful answer. 'Come on, Amber, tell me. I'm listening.'

'Dislike. Desire…' Amber frowned as she tried to make sense of the emotions inside. She had never imagined she could possess such a burning cauldron of mixed feelings about another human being. *This* human being. All her life, all twenty-two years of it, and she had never experienced such depth and violent strength of feeling. With her father there had been immense love, but it had been trusting and childlike and immensely soothing. This man didn't inspire anything like that. 'I hate you,' Amber croaked, 'and yet…' Her voice trailed to a halt; her shoulders drooped with tiredness.

'And yet…' His voice was soft and low. 'I'm sorry. I've put you through hell today, haven't I? One test after another.' Michael lowered his mouth and dropped a kiss onto Amber's partly open mouth. The warmth of his lips, the taste of him almost made her forget what he'd said—almost.

'*Test?* You mean…?' She shook her head, hardly able

to voice her suspicions. 'The urgent phone calls, the work to chase up, the report? And if I *had* gone straight upstairs?' she queried finally.

'But you didn't.'

'But if I had,' Amber repeated stonily, 'what then? Would you have exerted some of that supreme control and asked me to leave? How dare you?' Amber gritted. 'How dare you use me like this?'

'I wasn't aware I had done any such thing. When?' Michael demanded. 'When have I used you? In the lift? In the hotel bedroom? This evening? You have an exceedingly short memory, Amber. I recall events a little differently.'

'Why are you playing games with me like this?' she demanded. 'Why?'

He searched her face. 'Because everything has happened so quickly,' he told her fiercely. 'Because you've sprung into my life out of nowhere. Because you're different from other women—'

'And those other women have always gone straight for the bedroom!' Amber snapped.

'Very few have ever been allowed through the front door!' Michael delivered harshly.

'So I should count myself fortunate, I suppose? To have been permitted to enter this prestigious sanctuary? What an honour!'

There was silence. He loomed above her. She could feel the pressure of his body, hard and muscular against her own. She gazed into dangerous blue eyes and wondered whether it was madness or courage that had prompted her to say such a thing.

'Now who's playing games?' he growled, surveying her with undisguised dislike.

This time his mouth descended with unforgiving intent. She didn't stand a chance against the power of his on-slaught. They kissed as if their lives depended on it. Their embrace was like a battle—fierce and unrelenting, a punishment for all that had gone before. His hands were rough as he caressed her, sliding up to cup each aching breast.

Amber responded with gasps of delight and he kissed her mouth again, plundering every secret corner, holding her, curving her into the contours of his hard masculine body.

His passion left her breathless. Amber shivered, a reaction of anticipation and delight, as Michael's mouth traversed her throat, her jaw, her face. Desire flared between them out of nowhere. Their argument was forgotten. Nothing mattered except the exquisite torture of Michael Hamilton's caress.

Amber closed her eyes as her limbs melted and her body stirred, and then opened them with a start, aware of the desire that was threatening to take a hold.

'Michael…'

She searched his face for reassurance and he gave it to her, kissing her lips, whispering gently, 'Trust me, sweetheart…always trust me…'

He lifted her into his arms then and carried her along the hallway, up the starkly painted stairs, along unknown passageways, until finally they reached their destination.

He touched her with urgent, searching fingers and she gasped aloud, pressing her face against his cheek, kissing him abstractedly, running her fingers through the silky darkness of his hair.

'No turning back,' he murmured huskily. 'Not now. Not ever.'

Amber didn't reply. She couldn't. She was lost in a maelstrom of sexual feeling and emotion. Her body ached with wanting him. She felt as if she had been waiting an eternity for this, and now that the moment had arrived she knew she wanted it more than she had ever wanted anything in her life before.

'Look at me.'

She did so, watching as he raised himself up to sit astride her body. He freed his tie, dragging it away from the collar of his shirt, discarding the latter with determined speed, revealing, like a glorious prize, the vision of his magnificent chest.

Michael gazed down into Amber's face as she feasted her eyes upon him, and she reached out and touched the place where dark hair roughened the skin, her fingers lingering on the well-formed pectoral muscles, the solid lines of his ribcage. And he covered her hands, pulling her forward so that she sat facing him, so that he could slip her blouse from her shoulders, remove the lace bra from her breasts.

Semi-naked, they faced one another, kissing passionately, relishing the anticipation of the moments to come.

After they had taken pleasure in discarding the rest of their clothes, they lay together on the bed, stroking and touching.

Amber had never imagined in her wildest dreams that her first full sexual experience could be so...so magical, so sensuous, so deliciously deliberate.

The first full thrust of possession. Powerful, all-consuming—everything Amber had ever imagined it would be. Pleasure, as he repeated the motion, and pain, but nowhere near as much as she had anticipated.

Sensation swamped her—powerful, abandoned, extravagant sensation. And glory. The wonder of sharing, of experiencing the ultimate in togetherness. They moved in urgent unison, limbs entwined, gripping, touching; fierce, hot kisses, groans of intense pleasure...

Afterwards Michael's mouth was warm against her neck. He stroked a strand of hair back from Amber's face and looked into her eyes. 'That was special,' he whispered huskily.

'Yes...' Her voice was unsteady. He was right. So right. She wanted to cry. And yet she didn't feel sad.

Michael stroked her face with a gentle finger and then kissed her mouth with infinite softness. 'It's not just about sex,' he murmured. 'You have to believe that.'

She wanted to—so much. But was Michael talking about making love in general, or referring to what had just taken place between them?

He gently lifted Amber from him. 'I'll run a bath,' he murmured, walking through to the *en suite* bathroom, which Amber could see from her vantage point on the king-sized bed. 'Don't run out on me now, will you?'

Amber smiled. 'The thought never crossed my mind,' she whispered honestly. 'I'm here for as long as you want me.'

They bathed together, the temperature rising perceptibly as Michael languorously soaped every inch of Amber's body.

Afterwards they lay together between fresh sheets, simply holding one another, kissing a little, listening to soft music on a discreet stereo that was tucked away on a shelf in the corner of the room.

'So how come you're a virgin—*were* a virgin?' Michael asked quietly. He held Amber close and looked deep into her eyes. He murmured softly, kissing her mouth, 'I can't understand how such a wonderful phenomenon could occur.'

'A *phenomenon—me*?' Amber queried lightly. 'I don't think so.'

'In this day and age?' He paused. 'How old are you?'

'Twenty-two.'

'You're a beautiful woman and you're not ashamed of your body. Yet you've kept that part of your life under wraps for a pretty long time,' Michael murmured. 'Hasn't there ever been anyone serious in your life?'

Amber shook her head. 'No.'

'I feel honoured.'

She twisted around to look up into the handsome face. 'Are you laughing at me?' she whispered uncertainly.

'No.' His steady gaze told her that what he said was the truth. 'I meant it. You've no idea how I felt when I discovered that I was the first.'

Amber sank her head back against the strongly muscled arms which held her and gave a little sigh. 'It was wonderful!'

'You know, you are doing spectacular things for my ego,' Michael drawled, kissing her mouth with languorous ease. 'We shall definitely have to repeat this performance.'

Amber smiled up at him. 'Promise?'

'Absolutely!' Michael rolled over in the bed and tugged her down with him so that she was pinned beneath his body. 'How about now?'

They made love as much if not more passionately than before. Each moment that passed saw Amber becoming a little less inhibited, a little more daring. To touch Michael as intimately as he touched her was a great joy, to see his response, to feel the urgency of his caresses.

When it was over he held her close and kissed her tenderly. 'I haven't felt this way for a long time. You make me very happy.'

'You mean that?' Amber whispered. 'I'm not just another one-night stand?'

'*Another?*' Michael's mouth twisted in a sardonic smile. 'Who says I've ever had any?' He dropped a kiss onto her trembling mouth, and when he spoke next his voice had taken on a more serious tone. 'We both need to understand that what's happened between us means something. We need to be able to trust one another. To know one another. To feel that there are no barriers between us. That's how any successful relationship thrives.'

Amber's eyes stung. 'You want us to have such a relationship?' she asked quietly, hardly daring to listen to the answer.

He surveyed her with a grave expression. It spoke volumes. 'What do you think?'

Guilt. Amber was consumed by it.

Her throat locked, and for one awful moment she thought she would burst into tears.

'You know, I have a real need to do something crazy!' Michael didn't seem to notice the stillness that had settled over her.

'Wasn't what we just did crazy enough?' Amber asked quietly. Oh please forgive me! she thought desperately. What have I done? What am I doing?

'This is serious, young woman!' he announced gravely. 'An event which doesn't occur very often is about to happen.'

'You mean like a comet appearing? That sort of thing?' Amber queried, determinedly thrusting away her fears and guilt, allowing herself to enjoy the spectacle of Michael Hamilton, empire-builder and entrepreneur, relaxed and looking incredibly happy.

'Exactly that, except maybe this event isn't quite so rare.' He kissed her lightly on the nose. 'I'm going to take tomorrow off. We are both going to.'

Amber frowned slightly, her mouth curving into a disbelieving smile. 'Just like that? But your appointments! Your work!'

'They can wait.' Michael's eyes devoured every inch of her face and she felt the thrill of desire all over again. 'It can all wait. Besides, I'm just being practical,' he added huskily. 'I don't think either of us would be able to concentrate particularly well. Between us we'd make one hell of a lot of mistakes!'

'This isn't one, is it?' Amber's voice was small, like a

child's. 'I mean us. This relationship. We hardly know each other and—'

Michael stifled Amber's escalating anxieties with another slow, lingering kiss. 'If it's a mistake, then it's one I'm going to enjoy making,' he asserted huskily. 'What about you?'

CHAPTER TEN

'HEY! Sleepyhead! Time to wake up!'

Amber opened her eyes, stirring lazily in the bed, and found herself gazing up into Michael's lethally attractive face. His dark hair was shiny and tousled and there was a rugged growth of beard shadowing his jaw.

She had had a disturbed night, scenes of treachery and deception dominating her dreams. The wisest thing would be to leave now, she told herself, but then Michael bent low and kissed her with erotic languor and all thoughts of leaving were banished from her mind.

'Go and have your shower and then I'll make us some breakfast,' he instructed. 'I want an early start.'

'Why?' Amber sat up in bed, hugging her knees, and watched as he walked back towards the bathroom and began lathering his face with soap. He wore only boxer shorts. His chest was magnificently sculptured and she longed to run her hands over it again, feeling the fall and rise, the well-defined outline of each and every muscle. 'Where are we going?'

'To the country.' He picked up a razor and concentrated on his reflection in the mirror, his large hands well practised at the task. 'I have a small place, not too far from London. I think you'll like it.'

Amber digested this new piece of information, enjoying the eminently male spectacle, feeling a burning glow of attraction and need inside. 'So this house...?' she mused, glancing around the tastefully designed bedroom.

'Is just for convenience's sake.' Michael manoeuvred the razor expertly over his chin. 'I travel far too many miles as it is.' He saw her smile and shake her head. 'What?' he demanded, frowning a little.

'Oh, I don't know…' Amber released a steadying breath. She felt fragile suddenly. The futility of the whole situation came rushing at her with a great amount of depressing force. 'Your life, it's so…so different.'

'And does that matter?' He looked at her, his blue eyes clear and sharp, even from this distance.

'How *do* you know I'm not just interested in you because of your money?' Amber asked quietly. 'Don't you have to be on your guard, watch out for gold-diggers, that sort of thing?'

'Perhaps.' He wiped his face with a towel and then draped it around his shoulders. 'And are you?' Smouldering eyes bit into her across the space of the bedroom.

'No…no, of course I'm not!' Amber replied swiftly. 'But that's just my word…' Her voice trembled noticeably. 'How do you *know*?'

'I don't, not for sure.' Michael lifted his shoulders in a slight shrug and smiled. 'I just have to trust you, to believe in you—in what we have together.' He dabbed the last traces of soap from his jaw with the towel. 'It's the only way. Or are you suggesting I hire a detective and ask for information about your background?'

He was joking, but his words still frightened the life out of Amber. She inhaled a steadying breath and forced herself to smile. She mustn't ruin this. However long it lasted, she had to make the most of this glorious happening. What was the point in feeling guilty and unhappy now? She must stop thinking of the futility of allowing herself to fall in love with such an emotionally self-sufficient individual.

Her heart thudded painfully in her chest. Falling in *love*? Was that what she had done? She felt slightly light-headed, almost sick with shock. Oh, goodness! Was it true? *Was* it? Couldn't it just be a case of infatuation or attraction or…or simple sexual desire?

No. Her head shook a little. It wasn't any of those things, she decided, and then she changed her mind and admitted that it was all of those things, but more—much, much more.

'Amber?' Michael's voice, deep and immensely attractive, cut into her thoughts. He was looking across at her. 'You look serious. Don't tell me you really are a gold-digger with her eye on the main chance!'

'I don't care about your money,' she replied with effort. 'That's not why I got involved with you.'

'So why, then?' He strolled over to the bed and sat down beside her. A large hand reached out and gently held her face. 'Tell me. Was it my charm? My incredible personality? What?'

He was teasing and that made everything a hundred times worse. He had no idea. Amber moistened her lips and wished she could just forget the fact that she'd ever had the ridiculous notion of hurting this man…of hating him.

Michael observed her silently for a moment and then he murmured, 'Is there something on your mind? If you're worried about our lovemaking, then don't be. I took precautions.'

'Oh!' Now she felt foolish, like a child. She hadn't given the practicalities a second thought. And that had been stupid of her.

He was still watching her. His voice was steady when he spoke, but there was an underlying tension in his question. 'You're not regretting this, are you? Because if you are then we should end it now, before—'

'No!' Amber's reply came straight from the heart. She released a taut breath, marvelling at her own selfishness. Hadn't she just been given an opportunity to finish this thing cleanly and with reasonable ease? 'No,' she repeated. 'Don't say that! I don't want it to end.'

'Well, smile, then.' Michael dropped a kiss onto her mouth. 'Make me believe it. I know you don't care about my money; if you did, you would never have brought the subject up.'

She made a great effort and tried to look happy. 'Have pity on me, sir!' Amber quipped. 'I'm just a poor East End girl who's had to struggle to survive!'

It was the right thing to do. The tension between them dissipated immediately. 'Great accent!' Michael's deep-throated chuckle made the effort it had taken to appear light-hearted and relaxed worthwhile. 'Are you really a cleverly disguised cockney?' he asked.

Amber shook her head. 'No. North London's more my territory.' She leant back in the bed and closed her eyes, concentrating. 'I could come from anywhere you like,' she told him. 'Go on, name some places.'

Michael looked puzzled. 'What?'

She forced herself to continue. 'A town, a country. Anywhere you like!'

He thought for a moment and then reeled off a list, whilst Amber obliged with a short reply in the relevant accent.

'You have a hidden talent,' he informed her with deliberate reverence. He reached for her hands and pulled her sharply from the bed. 'I'm impressed.' He kissed her mouth softly, slowly, and Amber's heart melted. 'Where did you learn to do that?' he asked huskily.

'Oh, it's just a knack,' she replied distractedly, linking her arms around his neck. 'I've built it up over the years. Different parts often need some sort of individual accent to make the character more believable—'

'Different parts?' Michael glanced down at her and frowned slightly. 'What are you talking about?'

She could feel herself paling visibly, then flushing as if her face were on fire. 'Oh...amateur dramatics,' Amber replied frantically. 'I'm quite keen.'

'Really?' He bent his head and brushed his lips against her own. 'You didn't put that particular hobby down on your application form. Are you any good?'

'Oh, no...' Amber shook her head. 'Pretty average.'

'You must let me know when you next perform,' Michael replied. 'I'll come along and lend my support.'

Her next performance? If only he knew! Wasn't she still giving the performance of her life?

No, she wasn't. In the beginning she had put on an act, but that had disintegrated long ago...a lifetime ago...

Fate was being cruel. She looked up at the stunning profile and felt the curl of desire deep in the pit of her stomach.

How could she have known she would end up loving him?

They kissed in the bedroom, in the bathroom whilst Amber was having a shower, and in the kitchen over breakfast. During the drive out of town their desire grew mile by mile.

They arrived at their destination around the middle of the morning. It was a glorious place, such a contrast with the dust and the noise of the city.

The Mercedes roared along a sweeping drive lined with mature trees and woodland flowers and was brought to a halt outside the most gorgeous house Amber had ever set eyes on.

'*Oh!*' It was all she could say in that first moment, at that first glimpse. She gazed through the windscreen in astonishment, looking up at the red-bricked house with its ancient tiled roof and lattice windows. She had never seen such a beautiful house situated in such a wonderful setting. 'Oh!' she repeated.

'Is that it?' Michael looked across at her and smiled. 'Just, "Oh"?'

'It's...wonderful.' Amber tried hard to put her thoughts

into words. 'This setting, the quaint village…the sweep of countryside…'

'Does that mean you like it?' Michael leant across the car and kissed her mouth, drugging her with the power of his sexuality. 'Then I can relax; I thought you might consider it ostentatious.'

'Oh, no, Michael, it's wonderful!' Amber got out of the car on legs that didn't quite feel as if they were capable of holding her, and stared about her in amazement. 'But how could you describe this as *small*?' she asked, staring up at the hugely impressive house ahead of them. 'Michael, it's practically a mansion!'

'Don't exaggerate.' He came and stood beside her, curling an arm casually around her shoulders, turning Amber's insides to jelly because the gesture seemed so right and so natural. 'It's not that big.'

'It's beautiful,' she murmured softly. 'The sort of place people dream about. You're a lucky man,' she added, glancing up into his face.

'Yes. I know.' He kissed her again. 'Come on, let's go inside.'

He led the way along a flagstoned path, beside mounds of shrubs and sweet-smelling flowers, towards a heavy wooden door that was clearly many hundreds of years old. 'I have someone come in regularly,' Michael informed her as he unlocked the door, 'to keep the place aired so that it's ready to inhabit whenever I feel like escaping from London.'

'Like today.' The tension seemed to be falling away from her. It was this place, she decided as she leant against the open doorway and looked back at the beautiful garden and the wooded approach beyond. 'It's like a fairy tale,' Amber murmured. 'So peaceful.' She glanced down at the crisp business suit she still wore because Michael had been so impatient to escape the city. 'I feel overdressed.'

He turned back, loosening his tie as he approached. 'We can soon do something about that,' he replied huskily as his seductive fingers unfastened the buttons of her blouse. 'Can't we?'

It was a truly luxurious house—tasteful, and definitely designed with relaxation and pleasure in mind. Amber loved every single thing about Michael's home, from the elegant but simplified design of the interior to the fierce way the shower zapped you with its spray, right down to the tiny green plants which had thoughtfully seeded themselves in the cracks in the paved courtyard.

He had a pool too, indoor or outdoor, with an ingenious roof which slid one way or the other depending on the weather and the time of year.

Amber, clad only in a T-shirt, lifted her face from the sun's rays and took a wild, running jump and splashed, childlike, into the water.

She felt wonderful. Better than she deserved, maybe. But dwelling on the deception of her involvement with Michael didn't bear thinking about at the moment. It had happened. She had made a foolish mistake in the beginning and there was nothing she could do to change that fact.

She turned and looked towards the side of the pool. He was pouring himself a drink. 'Aren't you going to come in?' she called. 'It feels absolutely incredible!'

'The view's pretty incredible too!' He smiled, his eyes lingering on the wet outline of the T-shirt Amber was wearing. 'I don't suppose you feel like coming out now?'

'But I've only just got in!' She followed his gaze and discovered she felt more daring than she ever would have imagined possible. 'If you like it so much, then you can have it!' she called, pulling the T-shirt over her head. 'Here!' She scrunched the material up into a ball and threw it in Michael's direction. Then she ducked below the surface and swam strongly underwater to the far side of the pool.

When Amber came up for air, breathing heavily, smoothing the wet strands of hair from her face, Michael was behind her. 'I like this swimsuit much better,' he drawled. 'It has a line, a glow of perfection that I find very stimulating.' She smiled, her body melting visibly as Michael's strong hands touched her. 'Do you know it's almost an hour since we made love?'

'Feels like a lifetime,' Amber murmured, gasping as he moved in close.

'Too long,' he agreed. 'I think we'd better do something about it, don't you?'

The day passed by in a haze of passionate intensity. They made love, they talked, they made love again. Sometimes they did the two things together, questions posed urgently by Michael as he rose above her, gasping answers returned by Amber who loved the domineering masculinity of his voice.

'If I ask you about all the golden-haired girls with smiling red mouths, will you be mad?' Amber murmured.

They were lying on a rug in the garden, hidden by a carefully orchestrated muddle of herbs and flowers and shrubs. Amber picked up a strawberry from the bowl which lay between them and dipped it into another which contained thick, fresh cream.

'Not mad, no,' Michael replied cautiously.

Amber scanned his handsome face. He had caught the sun, just as she had; his skin was a rich golden bronze. On impulse, she reached out a hand and gently touched the side of his face. 'What, then?'

'Reticent, maybe.' He shrugged. 'What would be the point?'

'You told me about them in the first place,' she pointed out. 'What was the point then? Just to make me jealous?'

'Were you?'

She looked at him calmly. 'Of course I was!' She swirled another strawberry around in the cream. She decided to plunge into dangerous waters; it was stupid maybe, but loving someone, as she was swiftly finding out, was never meant to be easy. 'I suppose they were all extremely beautiful,' she murmured.

'Beauty isn't everything.' There was a slightly tense pause. 'In fact,' Michael continued, 'appearance in the long-term counts for very little. You may *think* you can judge a book by its cover, but of course it's impossible.'

'What do you mean?' Amber asked quickly. 'Are you talking about me?'

'You?' He frowned, and she saw instantly that she had overreacted, been too sensitive because of the guilt that was festering away inside. 'Why should I be talking about you?' Michael enquired evenly. 'Are you trying to tell me you've got something to hide?'

This could be it. She could speak up now, confess, *finish* everything.

'You *were* right...' She tried to smile and failed miserably. 'It was a silly subject to drag up. I shouldn't have asked.'

'No,' Michael agreed. 'You shouldn't. So...' He caught Amber's wrist and guided her hand to his mouth, plucking the strawberry from her fingers with his teeth. 'Let's talk about something else. You. Tell me something interesting, something I don't know.'

Her heart thudded violently in her chest. She wasn't out of the woods yet—but when would she ever be? To deceive him so—what had ever possessed her?

'What can I say?' she murmured evasively. 'There's little of the first and not a great deal more of the second. Honestly,' she added lightly, aware of Michael's intense gaze, 'you'd be bored to tears in no time!'

'Try me.'

He wasn't used to being deflected from a subject that he had set his heart on. Amber shook her head, her eyes widening in appeal. 'I'd much rather do something else,' she declared fervently.

Michael leant forward and kissed her mouth. 'From virgin to nymphomaniac,' he teased huskily. 'Do you think, as teacher, I should feel guilty?'

'Not at all.' She dipped her finger into the cream and then pressed it against Michael's smiling mouth. 'Teach me some more.'

'Don't think I won't find out everything there is to know about you,' he drawled, running a sensuous hand over Amber's heated body, 'because I will. But later...much later...'

It was early evening. Amber was wrapped in a huge towelling robe. She sat at the desk in the downstairs drawing room and quickly wrote the letter which she had been composing in her head whilst she had stood under the shower.

Guilt was eating away at her happiness. She had tried not to let it, but it was more powerful than her will—than her own selfishness. Writing the facts down calmly would help. Adding her feelings would probably be pointless, but she had to do it. She wasn't exactly sure how or when she would tell Michael about Beatrice, and her own misguided decision to seek revenge, but she would do it—and sooner rather than later. For his sake as well as her own.

She heard Michael's footsteps on the stairs and hurriedly folded the piece of paper, thrusting it into an envelope which she pushed into the spacious pocket of her robe.

'What are you doing down here?' He looked intrigued. He leant against the doorjamb, a vision of incredibly sexual masculinity. Biceps firmed and bulged as he folded his arms across his bare chest. A towel was slung low on his hips, revealing the taut, flat planes of his stomach. He smiled and Amber's heart melted. 'I thought you were going to wait for me upstairs.'

'I...I thought I heard a noise.' She hated lying but she had to improvise quickly. 'I decided to take a look.'

'In here?' Michael frowned and glanced around the room. 'What sort of noise?'

'It was nothing!' Amber replied swiftly. 'I was mistaken.'

'You look tense.' Michael walked towards her and tugged her against his muscled frame with obvious intent. He rested his hands on her shoulders and began massaging slowly and with great effect. 'Just feel those knotted muscles,' he murmured. 'What's the matter?'

'I...I'm a bit tired, that's all.'

'Honestly?' Melting blue eyes held her face. 'So you're exhausted? And I'm to blame—all this physical activity. It's a hell of a way to keep fit!' His mouth slanted. 'You realise that there's absolutely no way that we're returning to London tonight?' he added, kissing her softly on the mouth, so that she had no choice but to melt into his arms. 'Of course, it all depends on how good you are this evening,' he added hypnotically. 'But we may even play hookey tomorrow as well.'

'What about the office?' Guilt was battling valiantly against personal desire, forcing her to put a few obstacles in the way.

'I'll drop down a notch or two in Miss Jones's estimation,' Michael drawled, 'but I think I can handle that.'

'There have been no phone calls,' Amber reminded him. 'I thought the line would be humming.'

'Miss Jones knows better than to disturb me here. My employees are nothing if not obedient,' Michael replied sardonically as he lifted her in one easy movement off her feet and into his arms. 'When I phoned her this morning, I told her it would have to be something pretty cataclysmic before I was contacted at all.'

'She's a loyal member of your team, isn't she?' Amber murmured quietly, remembering Beatrice's tearstained face.

'About as loyal as they come,' Michael agreed, carrying her across the room and through the doorway.

'I've often wondered why you didn't appoint her as your personal assistant,' Amber murmured, 'when your last one left so suddenly.'

'Because she's got an elderly mother who takes up every spare minute of her time, that's why—and because she's nowhere near as attractive as you are.'

'And your former personal assistant—wasn't she attractive?'

Michael paused at the foot of the stairs. He looked down into her face, watching, wondering at the seriousness of Amber's expression. 'She had a pleasant face, a nice personality,' he replied evenly. 'I was sorry to see her go.'

'Were you?'

'What are we talking like this for—so serious all of a sudden?'

Amber summoned every ounce of will-power she possessed and continued the theme. 'You must get a tremendous feeling of power, being in charge of your own company, holding so many people's futures in your hand.'

'Now you're making me sound like a megalomaniac!' Michael frowned as he lowered her to the floor. 'Amber, what is this?'

He really was becoming suspicious now. Maybe, deep down, that was what she wanted. 'I…I just wondered what it must be like to be in your position,' she replied quickly. 'Over a thousand employees…' Her voice drifted to a useless halt.

'Give or take a hundred.' She knew he was watching her

expression carefully. 'Care to tell me where this conversation is leading?' he asked quietly.

Amber flashed him a quick, unhappy glance. She couldn't push the subject any further. She wasn't brave enough. She was too frightened of losing what she had.

And what is that? Amber asked herself. You love Michael with every piece of your soul, but what does he feel for you? He loves your body—he clearly can't get enough of that—and he finds your company pleasant, but that's as far as it goes. There has to be more than that to sustain a relationship. Why can't you be honest with yourself? a silent voice yelled inside. Stop hoping. Stop *dreaming*!

'It's not leading anywhere!' She turned from him and began walking up the stairs towards the bedroom. 'I was just being incurably nosy.'

'No, you weren't.' Michael's footsteps sounded ominous behind her. He caught hold of her arm as they reached the bedroom door and spun Amber around. 'There's more to it than that,' he asserted grimly. 'I can see it in your face. Go on!' He threw her a steely look—the sort of look that would make a thousand employees quail. 'Stop gazing at me with those big golden eyes for a moment and say what you want to say!'

'Michael...please!' Amber's expression was full of appeal. 'Look, it doesn't matter!' She closed her eyes and shook her head in despair. 'It doesn't!' She pulled her arm free from his hold and ran into the bedroom.

'If that's the case, then why are you so upset?'

She glanced across the room. Michael was watching her intently—so intently that it made her want to cry. She shook her head, gulping a lungful of air. 'I never imagined things would work out this way,' she croaked. 'I thought I'd hate you. I *did* hate you at first...'

'You're not making any sense. Is this about us?' Michael demanded. 'Are you trying to tell me you regret—?'

'No!' Amber shook her head. 'No…' Her voice trailed away miserably. She closed her eyes and willed herself to be strong. She thrust her hands into the pocket of her robe and felt the sharp edges of the envelope.

'Do you forgive people who make mistakes?' she whispered.

'This *is* about us,' Michael replied slowly. 'Come here!'

'No.' Amber's voice was trembling badly.

'You're defying me?' He looked faintly amused.

Her blood simmered a little. 'It surprises you that I should?' she queried. 'You *want* me to be frightened of you, is that it?' she persisted.

'Hey! Hey! What's got into you?' His expression held incredulity as well as surprise. 'You honestly think I'm that sort of man? Some sort of tyrant who like to impose his will on other people?'

'You have a strong personality,' Amber replied. 'You can't deny that.'

'Nor would I want to. Something's happened,' he said quietly. There was a pause. He waited patiently for Amber to reply. 'But you're not going to tell me what,' he murmured slowly. 'Now, why is that, I wonder?' His gaze was savage and full of contempt. He turned from her.

'Michael!' Amber whispered tearfully.

But it was too late. He had left the room.

She awoke some time later. There was a hint of dawn in the sky. Amber stared for a moment at the vague outline of the trees and then turned slowly towards the middle of the rumpled bed.

He wasn't there.

Frowning, she raised herself onto her elbows, clutching

the single layer of sheet around her naked body, and looked across the room.

A lamp was burning dimly in the adjoining dressing room. Silently, she swung her legs off the edge of the bed and walked naked to the door.

'What are you doing?'

Michael looked up at the sound of her voice. His expression was almost blank, Amber noted with a sudden chill, as if she were the last person he had expected to see or hear.

'Nothing.' His eyes flicked to her face. 'Thinking a little.' He picked up a cut-glass tumbler from the table beside his chair and raised the liquid to his lips.

She stifled a yawn. 'What time is it?' she asked cautiously.

'Around three...four, maybe.' Michael lifted his broad shoulders in a shrug. 'I really have no idea.'

Amber scanned the carved profile. She couldn't read anything in the taut, enigmatic expression. She had been having a dream—a wonderful dream about Michael and herself and the future. She desperately wanted it to come true. Her eyes left his face after a moment, lingering of their own accord on the broad expanse of tanned flesh visible beneath the carelessly tied robe. 'Haven't you slept?' she whispered.

'No.' He took another mouthful of alcohol, tipping his head back to drain the glass. He looked across at her, his eyes surveying her shapely figure, lingering impassively on the body he had possessed so effectively only a few hours ago. 'Put something on. You'll get cold.' His voice was low and controlled, such a cool contrast to the way it could be. Amber shivered. 'There, you see?' he added roughly. 'What did I tell you? Go back to bed!'

'Will you come too?' She knew her voice sounded small and childlike, but there was nothing she could do about it. Her pride was worth the sacrifice; lying alone in the bed, crying herself silently to sleep—what would that prove? All she wanted was for Michael to hold her again, love her, so that this growing feeling of anxiety and hopelessness could be dispelled from her heart.

'In a while.'

'You look tired.' She took a pace or two towards him. 'Michael…I'm sorry about before. So sorry… Please…let's be together—'

'I said in a while!' His voice was like a whiplash, throwing her off balance, shocking her into taking a pace back against the wall.

Amber stared at the harsh mouth and felt her own quiver in response. 'Hell! Hell!' Michael rose in an instant from the chair and came to her, tugging her close against his body, pressing his face into her hair. 'I'm sorry…I didn't mean to shout like that.'

'But you did.' Amber's voice was flat. 'I think it would be best if I left—that's what you want, isn't it?' she added quietly. 'You've taken me to your bed, you've heard me beg and now you want me to leave.' She flexed her body and tried, without success, to release herself from Michael's grasp. 'Is it disappointment that makes you look so miserable?' she continued hoarsely, tipping her head back to look into his face. 'I didn't put up much of a fight, did I? No different from the other girls you told me about. Did you have such high hopes?'

'Be quiet!' He gripped her face with steely hands. 'You don't know what you're saying! This isn't a *game*!'

'Isn't it?' She stretched her lips into a smile that held absolutely no amusement. 'You've never hidden your intentions or tried to deceive me. I should have expected this—I did expect this. Let me go,' she added quietly. 'I'll get my clothes and leave. I deserve this. You've no idea how much—'

She heard the savagery of his curse and then Michael

was lowering his head and halting her breathless words with a kiss that held no illusion of tenderness. Smouldering tension vibrated from every pore of his body as he plundered her mouth with his harsh, searching lips.

'Every other time has been for both of us—this time is just for me!' he growled savagely, tugging away the belt at his waist.

But he was wrong. So wrong.

His passionate intensity, his anger only served to heighten Amber's awareness of him. All the misery and fear and guilt was banished as he continued to ravish her, as his hands demanded her body, moulding and caressing each and every part.

He took her there and then, pressing her against the wall, curving her body into his, groaning in harsh satisfaction as they both reached a swift and shuddering climax.

'You honestly believed that what had gone before would be enough?' he demanded breathlessly, eyes lingering intently on her flushed face. 'You imagined for even one second that I would be satisfied with one single, solitary night?'

Amber's eyes clung to the compulsive attraction, the gleam that was total male dominance. His gaze mesmerised her; she felt curiously moved by the shimmering, intense anger. 'Kiss me again,' she whispered.

He lowered his head then and brushed his lips against her mouth with a gentleness that belied the previous erotic savagery. He touched her. He used his knowledge and expertise to find the places that made Amber gasp and moan, that found her clutching at his body in impatience, holding him tightly, because deep down...deep down she knew that one day he would leave her.

Their lovemaking was all that she had ever dreamed about and more. It felt like the first time and the last time all rolled into one, and afterwards, a long time afterwards, when the sun had begun to rise over the horizon, Amber buried her head in Michael's shoulder and held him as if he was her salvation in a world full of danger and calamity. Her lifeline. Her future. Everything...

CHAPTER ELEVEN

'I DIDN'T mean to sleep so late. You should have woken me!' Amber clutched the sheet around her naked body and crossed the verdant expanse of lawn. Michael was standing with his back to her, gazing out at the roll of fields and woods which lay between his house and the village.

'You're dressed for the office. Has something happened?' She felt bright and hopelessly happy. Even if they did have to return to London, she didn't mind. After the events of last night she knew that the only thing that mattered was that they were together. 'Don't tell me—Miss Jones has called and it's something cataclysmic!' She had half run, half skipped across the lawn, revelling in the feel of the damp grass beneath her feet.

If Michael had turned to face her, he would have seen the beauty of the scene; Amber's auburn hair, tinged with streaks of gold, glinted alluringly in the morning sunshine, her lightly tanned body, the smooth, unblemished skin of her neck and shoulders a contrast against the whiteness of the sheet. Behind lay his house, magnificent amongst the lush greenery of the garden.

If he had turned to face her. But he didn't.

'Michael?' Amber called his name cautiously, slowing her pace, taking a few tentative steps towards him, frowning a little, hating the way her stomach churned and her body began to tremble. 'Have you…got to go back?' she repeated.

He didn't reply.

She went and stood beside him, trailing the sheet along behind her like the train of a wedding gown, and looked up at his strong profile. Something *was* wrong; she realised that as soon as she saw his face. She watched with a sinking heart as he thrust a hand into his jacket pocket and pulled out a long, slim leather-bound case.

'Here. Take this.'

'But…what—?'

'Just take it!'

Her mind remained obstinately blank. She wouldn't think about what might have happened to make Michael look so…so forbidding, so harsh. She stared down at the elegant jeweller's box in silence, turning it over and over in her hands.

'Aren't you going to open it?'

'What is it?' Amber clumsily held the linen sheet against her naked body, glancing down at the box in her hands, not sure what she should do—suddenly not sure about anything.

'You'll discover that when you lift the lid. Until an hour ago, it was a gift,' Michael added, with clipped precision. 'Now maybe it would be better described as payment for services rendered.'

'What services?' She did frown now, genuinely puzzled by his words. Why was he being like this? Hadn't everything been put to rights last night? Michael had held her like a lover who cared—no words of endearment, but caresses that surely couldn't lie? He had wanted her with a fierceness that had moved her to tears of joy. They had wanted each other. But now, seeing the firm, unforgiving mouth, the icy blue gaze that looked bleak and daunting and gazed far ahead into the distance…she wasn't so sure. Fears began to escalate in her mind. Dreadful fears…

'Open it!' His voice was harsh.

Amber swallowed, her eyes wide and rigid in an attempt to stave off the tears. 'Michael…' She shook her head, hardly able to voice her concerns. Then cautiously, because there seemed little else she could do, she prised open the two halves of the gilt-edged case.

Amsterdam...the jeweller's...a very special necklace that she had only ever dreamed of possessing... It all came flooding back as elegant diamonds and rich green emeralds twinkled up at her. Amber glanced up at Michael and shook her head in speechless astonishment.

'Don't insult me by pretending to refuse them!' he asserted sharply. 'You probably want them as much as you've wanted anything in your life before!'

'Don't tell me what I want!' She couldn't bear the hated tone of his voice a moment longer. She walked around and stood in front of him. 'Why are you looking at me like that?' she asked croakily. *Why?*'

'You can ask *that*?' he muttered fiercely, glaring down into her face. 'Surely you don't take me for a *total* fool?'

The tears began to trickle silently down her cheeks. Amber wiped them away with the back of her hand and then snapped the case shut, shaking her head miserably, holding the object out to him with hands that trembled quite violently. 'I don't want it.'

'Take it!'

No!' Her voice almost broke, but she kept her gaze firm, persisting with her outstretched hand. 'You can't make me,' she whispered eventually, lowering her arm, dropping the case onto the short green grass.

'But I'm your employer,' he drawled in a cruelly sardonic tone. 'Don't try and pretend that that detail had slipped your mind! After all, it's the very thing that brought us together in the first place.' He threw her a hard, savage look that left Amber trembling. 'The collision on the steps was rather well planned—not particularly subtle, but well thought out all the same—'

'No!' she cried. 'No, it wasn't like that! Please! Let me explain!'

'There's no need.' His voice was devoid of feeling, empty and cold, hating her. 'I know,' he added, after a momentary pause. 'I know everything.'

Her heart plummeted like a stone. Down and down into the icy, frozen depths where all her worst fears and nightmares lurked. She felt cold and then she felt hot. Nausea overwhelmed her and for a few seconds Amber actually thought she was in danger of being sick. She stared up in horror at Michael's unforgiving face. 'Please!' she whispered. 'Don't look at me like that! *Michael*...' She shook her head frantically, her golden eyes pleading with him. 'It's not how it must seem!'

'Isn't it?' He looked at her with a stony indifference which was worse—*much* worse—than anything Amber could have imagined. 'Do you expect me to believe one word, *any* word, you have to say?' he enquired in clipped, controlled tones. He took a pace away from her as if her proximity was too much to bear. 'I have to give you credit, though,' he continued in a deceptively mild tone. 'You played it cleverly. Not too eager, innocent when it suited, fiery, stubborn, sweet. A really intriguing mix.' Blue eyes scoured Amber's face. 'Quite a performance. How long did it take to get that character off pat?'

'It wasn't a performance!' Amber scrambled a few steps after him as he turned to cross the lawn and head back towards the house, dragging the sheet with her as she went. 'Do you honestly believe I could act everything out so callously?' she asked. 'Michael, please!' she called as he continued his relentless march. 'Can't you even listen?'

'What have you got to say that I don't know already? You're a determined character. You went to the trouble of forging your references, of lying your way into my employ—'

'That was in the beginning!'

'Just a few days ago!' Michael thundered, his voice lashing into her, as he turned back to face her. 'Don't insult me by pretending anything has changed!'

'I love you!' Her words came from the heart. Every ounce of feeling she possessed for him, every thought, every longing—all of it revealed in those three words which drifted across the lawn and were lost in the warm spring air.

It was all disregarded with a look of sheer and utter contempt. He shook his head as if he could hardly believe she had had the nerve to say such a thing. 'Get dressed!' he ordered. 'I want you out of this house as soon as possible.'

She stopped. Suddenly her legs didn't have the strength to hold her any more. She sagged to her knees, staring in dismay. He had judged her and she was guilty. 'You aren't going to let me explain? Please, Michael! Don't do this to me!'

'And what do you think you've done to me? I know it all!' He retraced his steps, standing a few feet from where she sat crouched on the grass. 'Beatrice Davies! Your stepsister!' His voice was clipped and without emotion. 'I know why you're here—what you hoped to achieve!'

'You've talked to her?'

'There was no need.' Michael shook his head.

'Well, how, then—?'

'Do I know?' His mouth twisted into an unhappy smile. 'The ever efficient Miss Jones. Your incompetence made her suspicious. She decided to double-check your references.' He gave a harsh laugh. 'She even went so far as to visit your good old friend in advertising, who was anxious to put the record straight as soon as the possibility of legal action was mentioned.'

'Miss Jones never liked me,' Amber murmured miserably.

'That's irrelevant! She found out the truth.'

'Michael please! Don't treat me like this!'

He walked past her and picked up the necklace from the ground. 'You have good taste,' he drawled. 'I had the jeweller in Amsterdam fly this over when we returned to England. I surprised even myself.' His mouth curved cruelly. 'It must have been our encounter in the lift.' Smouldering blue eyes burnt into her, forcing back the memories. 'The look of disappointment on your face when I told you we had to stop...'

He inhaled a sharp breath and swung away from her. 'I want you to think of me when you wear it,' he continued caustically. 'Look upon it as a keepsake, a reminder of a pathetically gullible man you once fooled so effectively.' He threw the case carelessly onto her lap and stalked towards the house. 'Get dressed!' he commanded. 'We're leaving!'

The ride back to London was a nightmare. Several times Amber tried to speak, but the words just wouldn't come. And anyway, what could she say? He knew the facts, and they couldn't be denied. What he didn't know was how she felt, how quickly she had discarded her original crazy idea, how swiftly she had found herself falling in love with him...

She felt worn out and frustrated. Totally shell-shocked by all that had happened. His anger had a debilitating effect on her. She was weak and he was strong. He only cared that she had deceived him. He didn't love her.

Michael dropped her off at her flat, staring straight ahead whilst she fumbled with the door. 'I'll have your money sent on,' he informed her tersely. And then the Mercedes was off, speeding down the untidy street, leaving Amber conspicuous and alone on the pavement with tears streaming down her cheeks.

She didn't step outside her flat for a week. She disconnected the phone and hibernated under the duvet, like an animal trying to heal its own wounds.

Even Beatrice couldn't get past the front door. She knocked for an eternity, long and loud enough at one point to necessitate Amber's having to speak to her, if only to reassure her that she was physically well.

She guessed, of course. Just a few incoherent sentences from Amber was all it took.

'I know I've been a fool!' Amber sobbed. 'You don't have to tell me that. I *know*! And I know you'll think I've made a dreadful mistake. But I love him and there's nothing I can do to change that fact.'

'You love him.' Beatrice repeated the words quietly. Amber glanced up. Curiously her stepsister's expression wasn't as horrified as she had expected. 'So what's happened?' Beatrice asked gently. 'Why are you in such a state?'

'Michael found out.'

That's all it took. Three simple words that told of the ruin of her life.

'And he thinks the worst?'

'He was *so* angry,' Amber sobbed miserably. 'I tried to explain, but he wouldn't listen. He…he said some horrible things.'

'You can't let him do this to you!' Beatrice cried, gripping Amber by the shoulders and giving her a none too gentle shake. 'He thinks the worst, but *you* know it's not true. Why are you lying down and letting him walk all over you like this?'

'He's not walking all over me,' Amber replied wearily. 'He's just cut me out of his life; it's as simple as that.' She inhaled an unsteady breath, rubbed a shaky hand over her red-rimmed eyes. 'Not that I was ever really a part of it. It all happened so quickly. Hours, days. That's how long we were together. It's nothing…nothing at all.'

'Does it feel like nothing?' Beatrice asked sharply. 'Is that why you've locked yourself away? Why you look like death warmed up? Because it was *nothing*?'

'No...' Amber gulped back a sob. 'I love him. You know I do...'

'Then do something about it! Tell him how it was—how it is now!' Beatrice cajoled fervently.

'I tried...' Amber shook her head, pressing her lips together manfully, because she was sick of crying all the time. 'He didn't want to know.'

'Maybe because he was really hurt, *is* still hurting,' Beatrice replied. 'He's a strong, hard and maybe ruthless man, but even men of that ilk can be capable of feeling pain.'

'He didn't look pained,' Amber murmured, remembering. 'He just looked angry.'

'I could try to see him,' Beatrice suggested suddenly. 'Would that help?'

'Oh, Bea, no!' Amber shook her head in disbelief. 'Please don't! It would be so awful for you!'

'Nowhere near as awful as you think.' Her sister frowned and looked uncomfortable. 'Look...I've...I've got something to tell you. I can't stand back and see you hurting so badly because of *me*. Oh, Amber! I'm so sorry! This is all my fault.' Beatrice shook her head, running her hands over her hair nervously. 'I never meant to allow things to go this far. I should have told you the truth in the beginning, but I couldn't bear it...' Her mouth twisted into a pained smile. 'I had been working too hard, was feeling stressed...' She paused. 'Rejection—none of us like it, do we?'

Amber frowned. 'Rejection? What...what are you talking about?'

'I lied,' Beatrice said quietly. 'I was so...so upset at the time. I felt foolish. I blamed it on Michael in part. I thought he had made me feel foolish, but he hadn't; it was all my doing.'

'Beatrice! Will you stop rambling?' Amber cried. 'What on earth are you talking about?'

'I had to leave, Amber, but not for the reasons I gave you.' Beatrice heaved a huge breath. 'Michael never tried to seduce me. I made that up. I don't know why. I don't know what on earth possessed me to say such a dreadful thing, but I did. I suppose it was because I could see that my feelings weren't reciprocated.'

'*Your* feelings?' Amber shook her aching head. This was almost too much to comprehend. 'Your feelings?' she repeated dumbly. She stared for a moment at her sister, trying to work everything out. 'Are you saying...that you felt attracted to Michael...and because he didn't feel the same way you—?'

'More than attracted.' Beatrice cut in. 'At the time...I was in agony. So close to him, day after day...'

'You were in *love* with him?'

Beatrice's face was a picture of torment. 'I thought I was, but I wasn't, not really. We were only ever employer and employee. It was a stupid crush.' Beatrice closed her eyes. 'Just a stupid crush. I know that now.'

'How do you know?' Amber's voice was sharp. This had come as a terrible shock. She couldn't believe Beatrice had done this to her, to Michael.

Beatrice opened her eyes, and Amber saw that they were sparkling suddenly. 'Because I've met someone.' She smiled hesitantly. 'He's special. More special than anyone else in the world. We're very happy.'

'Well, that's all right, then, isn't it?' Amber couldn't keep the edge from her voice—she was no saint and she didn't feel like acting like one. 'You're happy. Great!'

'And you can be again!' Beatrice replied swiftly. 'Go to him. Explain. Tell him how much you love him.'

'I've told him.' Amber's voice was flat. 'He doesn't care.'

'He cared before. He won't have stopped caring overnight.'

'It's been over a week,' Amber murmured miserably.

'Go to him.' Beatrice insisted. '*Make* him understand.'

So Amber did. After her conversation with Beatrice, she realised she owed it to herself, to her relationship with Michael—for it *had* been good, and could be so again, if only he'd allow it...

Amber walked up the steps of the Hamilton Corporation's offices and into the foyer. Rumour mingled with hard fact, which no doubt had been circulated by the faithful Miss Jones, was undoubtedly the reason for the stares of a few employees, but she didn't care. What other people thought about her was the least of her worries; what Michael thought about her—that was all that mattered.

Her old security pass gained her access. Amber refused to allow her mind to wander as she took the many stairs up to the top of the building. No lifts for her. Not today. Probably never again.

Fate was being kind. Miss Jones was away from her sentry post. Amber glanced at the desk that had been hers just a few days ago and saw that it was in the same mess as she had left it.

Her heart was pumping, her palms were moist and clammy and her fingers trembled when she lifted them to knock briefly on Michael's office door.

She had taken this decision to try to see him one more time mainly because of what Beatrice had said. The love she felt for him *was* worth fighting for. She couldn't just accept the way things had ended between them. She owed it to herself and to the man she had deceived to make him hear the truth. Maybe this time he'd listen and under-stand...

She heard his voice, the terse command to enter, and almost turned and fled, but some kind of masochistic, inner determination drove her on.

Michael turned as she entered, a slight hesitation in his movement the only sign that her appearance had any effect.

Amber had reverted to herself, dressed with deliberate defiance in faded denims and a simple white T-shirt, her bronze hair allowed to run riot over her shoulders in a blaze of glorious colour. Little make-up—just mascara and a smear of lipgloss.

'Coming to see me is a futile gesture.'

His voice was rigid. If it had been smooth and relaxed she might have admitted to the futility of her journey, but Amber might latch onto this overtly tense statement as a drowning woman latches onto a piece of floating driftwood. Surely it was a sign that he hadn't forgotten, that it hadn't been a case of out of sight, out of mind, that he still *felt* something, even if it was just overwhelming rage? Surely, she told herself as she stood trembling before him—surely that fierce, scowling look was better than nothing?

'I can't believe you mean that.' Her voice was little more than a whisper.

'What do you want?' He looked so formidable. Immaculately dressed in a dark business suit, powerful, handsome...the man she loved, would never, *could* never stop loving, despite everything.

Amber swallowed; her stomach was churning uncontrollably now and she panicked slightly, conscious that time was short and every word which passed her lips mattered dreadfully. 'To be allowed to explain,' she replied quietly. 'Please believe me when I tell you that all I've done is go over and over the mistakes I made.' Golden eyes narrowed in anguish. 'I know I was a fool. But's that me...I don't think. I just feel. And Beatrice was so upset and I was so angry because—'

'Because of me.'

'Yes.'

'You're telling me things which I already know. You entered my employ to enact some sort of pointless revenge.'

'It wasn't pointless to me,' Amber replied.

'You see?' Michael lifted his hand in an angry gesture. 'You admit it! What else is there left to say?'

'There's more! Of course there's more! Do you always see everything in black and white?' Amber enquired angrily. 'Surely...*surely,* after the way things have been between us, you can allow me this opportunity to explain?'

She watched fearfully as Michael rose from behind his desk and walked over to the window, pausing to glance down at the busy London street below. Then he turned to face her, icy blue eyes resting on her face impassively, and for a moment she still wasn't sure, feeling like a condemned prisoner still desperately hoping for a last-minute reprieve.

'Very well,' he said quietly. 'I'm listening.'

Amber's heart thudded. Here was the opportunity she had been praying for, but fear overwhelmed her. She loved him so much and she was so frightened of saying the wrong thing, of blowing this one last chance to make Michael understand.

'It wasn't planned,' she murmured. 'You must believe that. At least...not what happened between us. I never expected—'

'By *it* do you mean the sex?'

Amber drew in a sharp breath and stared across the large office at Michael. Did he really intend that she should suffer like this? she wondered. Was he only allowing her to stay so that he could make the pain worse? Her eyes filled with tears. She hesitated for a long moment, desperately trying to work out how she should continue. 'Don't, *please!*' she whispered, imploring him with her eyes. She gulped a swift, uneven breath. 'You must understand…Beatrice was so unhappy,' she murmured quietly. 'Absolutely distraught.'

'Am I supposed to be interested this?' Michael demanded. 'Your sister chose to resign for reasons best known to herself!'

'Please listen!' Amber replied fretfully. 'Don't you give anyone a second chance?'

He threw her a cold look. 'It depends on the size of the crime.'

'Beatrice resigned because she thought she was in love with you,' Amber informed him wildly. 'She couldn't face the fact that your interest in her was purely professional. That's why she left so suddenly. And she told me…' Amber's voice faltered for a moment. 'She told me that you had tried to seduce her, that you were cold and hard and unforgiving when she refused.'

'She did *what?*' Michael thundered, his expression revealing something other than stony indifference at last.

'She knows she did wrong,' Amber replied swiftly. 'She's beside herself with remorse.'

'And you believed all that she told you.'

'I didn't know you then!' Amber cried. 'And Beatrice is my stepsister.'

'So, now you know the truth.' His voice was full of wintry calm. 'What a shame all your efforts weren't for a good cause!'

'You think I slept with you because of…of…?'

'Revenge?' Michael lifted his shoulders in an uncaring shrug. 'It sounds ridiculously dramatic, doesn't it? But then,' he added pointedly, 'you're a particularly dramatic girl.'

'Michael!' Amber shook her head in dismay and took a few steps towards him. 'Please don't look at me like that! Don't you see? I never wanted to fall in love with you.'

'Is that supposed to make me feel better?' he enquired caustically.

'But don't you see? It just…happened!'

'And you chose to keep up the deception? I find that hard to believe. You lied!' he accused. 'You deceived me!'

'When I realised how I felt about you…' Amber shook her head frantically. 'I was weak. I know I was. I didn't want to lose you!'

'What makes you think you ever had me?' He turned once again to the window. 'Remember what I said to you about the women in my past?' The dark head shook. 'I thought you were different…'

There was a telling pause. Silence engulfed the room. 'I think we've covered all there is to say!' Michael turned back towards Amber and his gaze was bleak. 'Let's just end this whole thing now while it's still dignified. I've learned, and so, if the look on your face is anything to go by, have you.'

She had failed. How could she possibly get through to someone who had closed down the shutters and retired behind a mask of impervious, unrelenting fury?

But she wouldn't go without a fight. She wouldn't let him do that to her. 'You think I care about *dignified*?' Amber strode towards him. Now it was her turn to be angry. 'A devious, manipulative girl like me, with her eye on the main chance? What a nice life you have, Michael Hamilton. So controlled. So ordered! But I got through that, didn't I? For a while you allowed me inside; you actually permitted someone to get close. That's what you can't take. You're frightened! Frightened of admitting that what we had was worth something. Well, you can't take that away from me!' Amber gulped a hasty breath. 'You can't! I said

I loved you and it's the truth. If you aren't brave enough to accept that fact then it's your loss as well as mine!'

She turned as her voice broke on a sob and walked on jelly-like legs towards the door, praying with all her heart that Michael would call her back.

Just as she was about to leave, he spoke. His voice was quietly intense. 'Do you know how much I'd like to believe you?'

Amber stopped and listened to the thud of her heart. Slowly—oh, so slowly—she turned and looked back to where Michael was standing. He hadn't moved. He looked as hard and unforgiving as ever, but she knew—she just *knew*—that now there was a chance.

'I wrote a letter to you,' she whispered. 'When we were together at the house. I wanted to explain things. To try and make you understand. I *was* going to give it you. But we were having such a wonderful time and I loved you so much...' Amber swallowed back the lump in her throat and sniffed hard. 'It's...it's in the pocket of the dressing gown I wore—or at least it should be,' she whispered fervently. 'If you read it you'll understand how guilty I was feeling, how mixed up and totally confused I was—*am*.'

'I know about the letter.'

'You do?'

'It's here,' Michael informed her neutrally. 'In my pocket.'

'But surely if you know how I felt—?' Amber began fervently.

'I haven't opened it.'

She frowned. 'Why not?'

'Because I didn't want to see the truth in black and white, that's why!' he thundered. 'I knew. As soon as I discovered it, I knew it was a confession—'

'It's more than that,' Amber whispered. 'It's a declaration of love.' Michael thrust his hands into his inner jacket

pocket and pulled out the crumpled envelope. 'Please...
open it,' Amber pleaded. She closed her eyes and felt a
peculiar weariness settle over her. Food hadn't been much
of a priority recently, and fighting a constant battle with
tears had taken its toll. 'I love you so much,' she repeated
quietly. 'More than you'll ever know...' And then she
crumpled to her knees, and with relief she saw that the
rolling, lurching sea of grey carpet was rising to meet her.

'Amber! Oh, sweetheart!' She heard a muttered oath that
sounded curiously like, 'I love you,' and her lashes flew
open.

Michael. Kneeling beside her, looking down into her face
with an expression that made her heart leap with joy. She
had heard his voice, those words... It wasn't an illusion,
was it? She reached out a trembling hand towards his face.
Had she heard correctly? Or was the pain and anguish of
loving him making her hallucinate?

'I love you,' Michael repeated softly, looking deep into
her tear-filled golden eyes. 'I don't think I can live without
you.'

She thought for a moment that she might faint. The world
seemed to become distant. The vision of the man she loved
receded a little into the distance as blackness closed in and
tried to blot him out. She reached out a hand and felt the
strength of his fingers gripping hers.

'It's OK,' he said strongly. 'Everything's going to be all
right. I'll get you some water.'

He was back in a moment, cradling Amber in his arms,
helping her as she took a sip from the glass he held to her
lips.

'Michael... ?'

'I meant what I said.' She looked into his eyes and saw
that it was true. The mask had finally been cast aside. She
saw the smouldering, dark intensity, the look of concern

and love in his expression. 'I've never meant anything so much in my life before.'

Tears spilled onto Amber's cheeks. She stared up in wonderment. That he should say he loved her, that he should look at her with such intensity...

Never, never in her wildest dreams had she imagined something as wonderful as this. Just to make him understand so that he didn't hate her was the best she had hoped for.

'Oh, *Michael*!' Amber shook her head in breathless astonishment. 'Oh, my darling! I hurt you and I'm so sorry!'

'I hurt you too. On that last morning...' The dark head shook as he remembered. 'I know I should have given you a chance to explain. I was hard and cold—'

'You were hurting.'

The compelling, attractive mouth twisted into a pained smile. 'Yes. But you didn't know how much.'

'I thought...I knew that you liked me...' Amber began.

'*Liked* you?' His mouth widened into a disbelieving smile. 'I adored you! I couldn't stop thinking about you! The magic between us was something that I had never experienced in my life before!' He looked concerned suddenly. 'Surely you felt it too?'

'Yes! Oh, yes!' Amber cried. 'But I had no faith...not in myself, especially not after the way I had deceived you.' There was a slight hesitation and then she added, 'Why...didn't you tell me how you felt?'

Michael searched Amber's pale face with a frown. 'You were right before. Fear hasn't been a part of my life—I've found myself able to cope with just about any situation that's come my way. But you...' he smiled gently '...or rather what you did to me, the way you made me feel...*then* I experienced fear. Always, *I've* been the one to control a relationship, but you turned me upside down, inside out.

'You said something on that last evening at the house about the fact that you'd *thought* you would hate me. I didn't understand what you meant. That's what I was brooding about in the early hours when you found me alone with my glass of whisky. I couldn't stop thinking about you...*wanting* you...imagining what it would be like should I lose you...' He inhaled a ragged breath.

'Then you came to me and we made love and I finally convinced myself that everything was going to be wonderful. On that last morning, I got up early. I felt so alive, so full of plans for the future. I was going to bring you breakfast in bed, give you the necklace...' There was a pause as he remembered, and his gaze became bleak. 'Then the phone rang and I found out that what I'd thought was going to be a routine piece of business was really a personal nightmare.'

Amber shifted in his arms. She sat up straighter, rigid with intensity. 'But you *do* understand now?' she asked. It was very important that he did. 'You understand,' Amber continued fervently, 'that I was foolish and stupid in the beginning, but that everything altered as soon as I met you?'

'I understand that when we met all our priorities changed,' Michael replied instantly. 'What had seemed important before no longer mattered. For you it was a madcap scheme to help your sister. For me...' He smiled and leant forward, kissing Amber softly on her mouth. 'For me...it was everything—my business, my life, my past...'

'I loved you in Amsterdam,' Amber whispered.

'I loved you on the steps of this building,' Michael responded huskily, drawing her even closer.

'I never planned that collision,' Amber whispered. 'It was just me being clumsy and cross.'

'Good.' Michael's hands caressed her face with infinite care, sweeping back the strands of her hair, his fingers stroking along the lines of her throat. 'I adore you that way.'

'I tried to be someone else,' Amber murmured. 'Someone smart and sophisticated. But it just never worked out, did it?'

'No.' His mouth curved into a devastating smile. 'And I'm glad.' He kissed her gently, convincing her. She felt the strength of him, the restraint that he was having to exercise as his mouth moved against hers, loved the sound of the reluctant groan as he finally ended their kiss. 'Will Beatrice be hurt when she finds out about us?'

'She already knows. Besides, she's met someone. She's very happy—or at least she will be when she discovers that you and I are friends again.'

'More than friends,' Michael asserted. 'Much more than that.'

'Can you ever forgive me for being so foolish?' Golden eyes lifted to his face.

'I can forgive you anything,' Michael informed her huskily. 'As long as you agree to something.'

'What?' Amber's joyful expression was tinged with puzzlement.

'It's quite a commitment,' Michael warned. 'It will entail great sacrifice and forbearance.'

'You don't want me to continue to be your personal assistant, do you?' she asked, frowning. 'I'm sorry, Michael, but, to be honest, I don't think I could handle another day working with Miss Jones—'

'Not that, no.'

Amber shook her head, revelling in the nearness of him, in the touch of his hands on her skin. She wanted him to make love to her. She wanted it so badly that it was like a yearning pain inside her. 'What, then?' she asked.

'Just one thing,' Michael murmured, brilliant eyes shimmering down at her. 'I want you to be my wife.'

EPILOGUE

THE tiny grey church was packed to capacity. Flowers filled every nook and cranny; creamy roses in the softest hues mingled with the delicate freshness of green ferns. Late October sunshine streamed through the stained glass windows, throwing coloured light onto the hushed congregation.

Amber glanced around her. She listened to the melodic tune as the organ heralded her procession up the aisle, heard the rustle of ivory satin on the scrubbed flagstoned floor at her feet, felt the glow of happiness inside her like a living thing and doubted that it was possible to be any happier than this.

Michael was ahead. Golden eyes rested longingly on the tall, strong figure, clad in the smart morning suit. He turned and looked at her, and she knew his smile was for her and her alone. *He loved her.* Amber could see it in his eyes, feel the passion and the warmth emanating from his body as she approached and stood alongside.

'You look wonderful,' he said softly, linking his strong, tanned fingers with hers. His mouth twisted into that familiar, devastating smile she knew so well, and his blue eyes crinkled mischievously. 'Marry me?'

Afterwards, in the glorious autumn sunshine, they drove the few hundred yards from the centre of the village to his home, *their* home.

On the sweeping lawn in the distance, the grand marquee awaited their arrival. Palest mint-green and white bunting wound its way through the trees as they travelled in the quaint horse and carriage along the sweeping gravel drive.

Amber twisted the simple gold band round and around her finger and found that she couldn't stop smiling.

'You're happy?'

Amber snuggled deeper against the protective strength of Michael's broad frame. 'More than you'll ever know,' she murmured, raising her face to his, kissing him softly on the mouth.

He smiled, blue eyes glittering down at her with passion and love. 'I think I might have a pretty good idea. On a scale of ten?'

'Twenty!' Amber replied, laughing. 'No, a hundred! A thousand!'

Michael reached forward and touched the delicate glittering necklace that lay at the base of Amber's throat. 'I'm glad you chose to wear it,' he told her huskily. 'I bought the necklace because I loved you then. Amsterdam—the city of diamonds.'

'We'll be able to visit the city again, won't we—on our honeymoon?' Amber asked.

'We'll make it our first port of call,' Michael promised. 'We could even visit old Harry Vincent and show him how clever we are, now that we're man and wife!'

'Seriously?'

'No.' Michael shook his head. 'Not unless you want to, that is.'

'I'm quite content knowing that he's well again,' Amber replied. 'And that he's happy with the way the takeover's been handled. You've kept on quite a few of his old employees, haven't you?' Amber smiled. 'You're not quite the ruthless operator I first imagined!'

'Me? Ruthless?' Michael's expression was one of feigned innocence. 'How could you ever believe such a thing?'

Amber beamed. 'My husband!' she pronounced happily, lifting a hand to touch Michael's handsome face gently. 'I can scarcely believe it. It's a wish come true.'

He gazed deep into her eyes. 'From this day forward until the end of time, I'll grant you any wish you desire!'

'*Anything?*' she teased. 'Anything at all? Will you work less hard?' she asked, suddenly serious. 'Will you take care of yourself, so that we can live a long and happy life together?'

'You're thinking of your father.' Michael's voice was husky against the bronze strands of her hair. 'I promise,' he whispered. 'I'll promise you anything.'

'I've never been on a world tour before,' Amber murmured, sighing happily, turning to link her arms around her husband's neck. Her eyes devoured the lethally attractive face and her heart melted with love. 'Is this really happening?' she whispered, looking deep into the azure eyes. 'Am I really your wife?'

'For ever and always,' Michael muttered fiercely. 'For ever and always.'

And then he took Amber in his arms and kissed her for a very long time.

And as the church bells rang out joyously and the guests, a smiling Beatrice among them, gathered on the lawn of their home, waiting to greet them, Amber knew she would remember this moment for as long as she lived.

HARLEQUIN PRESENTS®

HARLEQUIN PRESENTS
men you won't be able to resist
falling in love with...

HARLEQUIN PRESENTS
women who have feelings
just like your own...

HARLEQUIN PRESENTS
powerful passion in
exotic international settings...

HARLEQUIN PRESENTS
intense, dramatic stories that will keep you
turning to the very last page...

HARLEQUIN PRESENTS
The world's bestselling romance series!

Harlequin® Historical

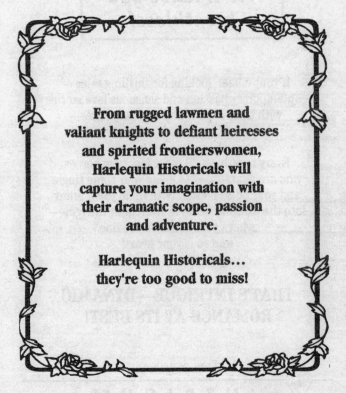

From rugged lawmen and
valiant knights to defiant heiresses
and spirited frontierswomen,
Harlequin Historicals will
capture your imagination with
their dramatic scope, passion
and adventure.

Harlequin Historicals…
they're too good to miss!

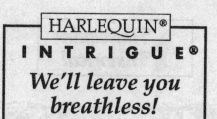

HARLEQUIN®
I N T R I G U E®
We'll leave you breathless!

If you've been looking for thrilling tales of
contemporary passion and sensuous love stories
with taut, edge-of-the-seat suspense—
then you'll *love* **Harlequin Intrigue!**

Every month, you'll meet four new heroes
who are guaranteed to make your spine tingle
and your pulse pound. With them you'll enter
into the exciting world of Harlequin Intrigue—
where your life is on the line
and so is your heart!

THAT'S INTRIGUE—DYNAMIC
ROMANCE AT ITS BEST!

 HARLEQUIN®

I N T R I G U E®

INT-GENR

HARLEQUIN® AMERICAN ROMANCE®

LOOK FOR OUR FOUR FABULOUS MEN!

Each month some of today's bestselling authors bring
four new fabulous men to Harlequin American Romance.
Whether they're rebel ranchers, millionaire power brokers
or sexy single dads, they're all gallant princes—and
they're all ready to sweep you into lighthearted fantasies
and contemporary fairy tales where anything is possible
and where all your dreams come true!

You don't even have to make a wish...
Harlequin American Romance will grant your every desire!

Look for Harlequin American Romance
wherever Harlequin books are sold!

HARLEQUIN SUPERROMANCE®

...there's more to the story!

Superromance. A *big* satisfying read about unforget-
table characters. Each month we offer
four very different stories that range from family
drama to adventure and mystery, from highly emo-
tional stories to romantic comedies—and
much more! Stories about people you'll
believe in and care about. Stories too
compelling to put down....

Our authors are among today's *best* romance writ-
ers. You'll find familiar names and
talented newcomers. Many of them are
award winners—and you'll see why!

If you want the biggest and best
in romance fiction, you'll get it
from Superromance!

Available wherever Harlequin books are sold.